☿MENAGERIE

ADULT ANTHROPOMORPHIC FOLIO 4

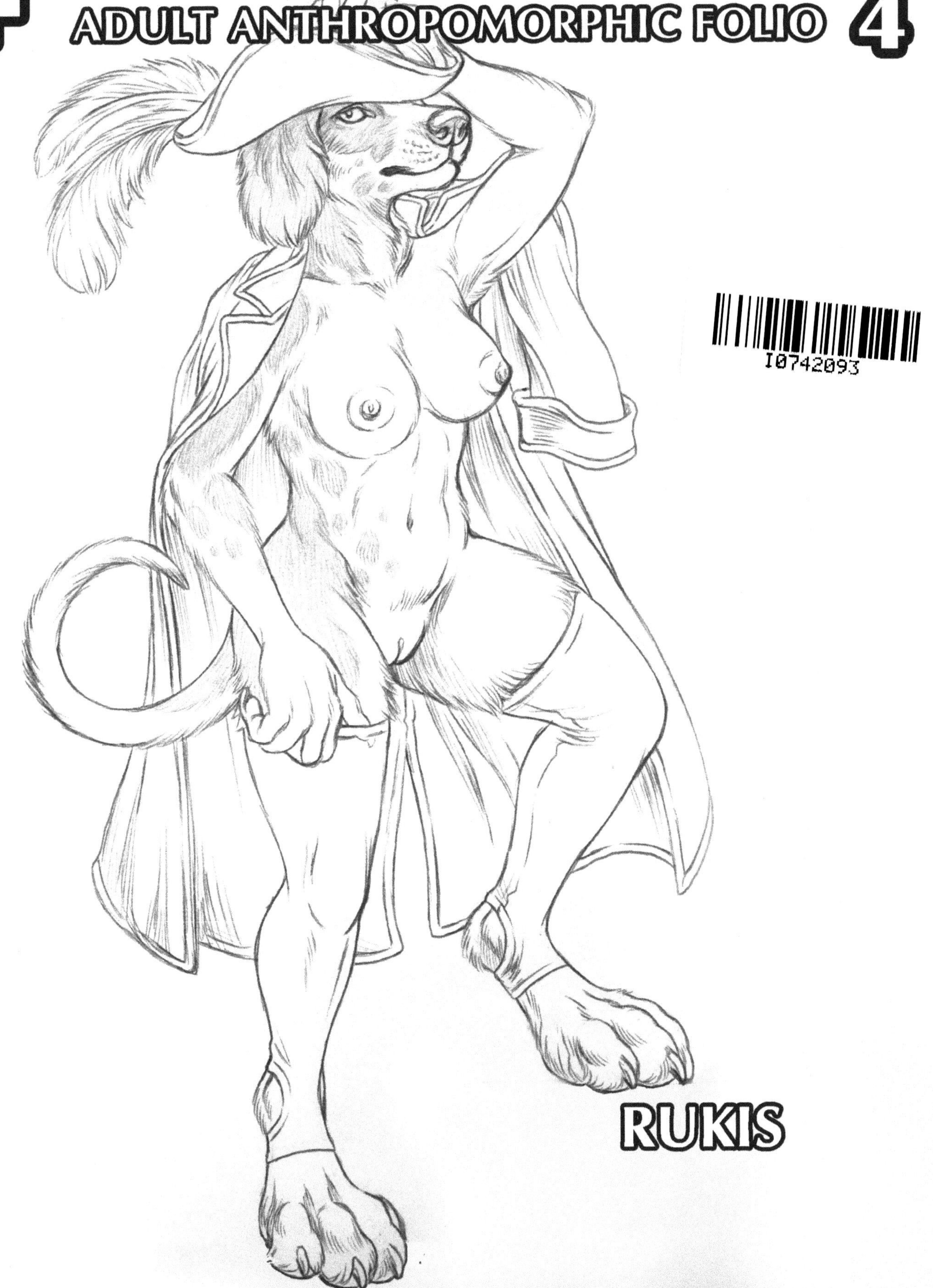

RUKIS

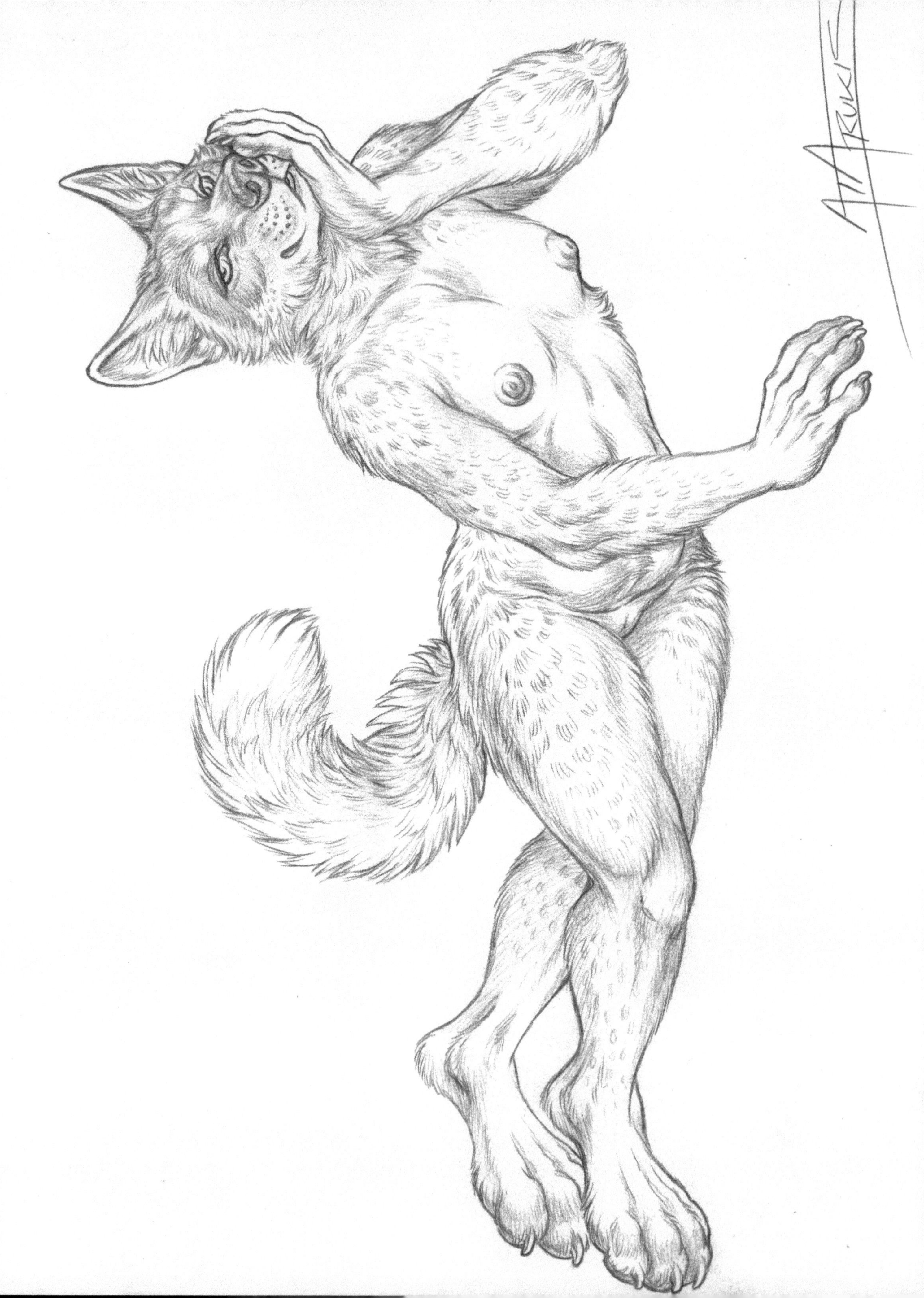

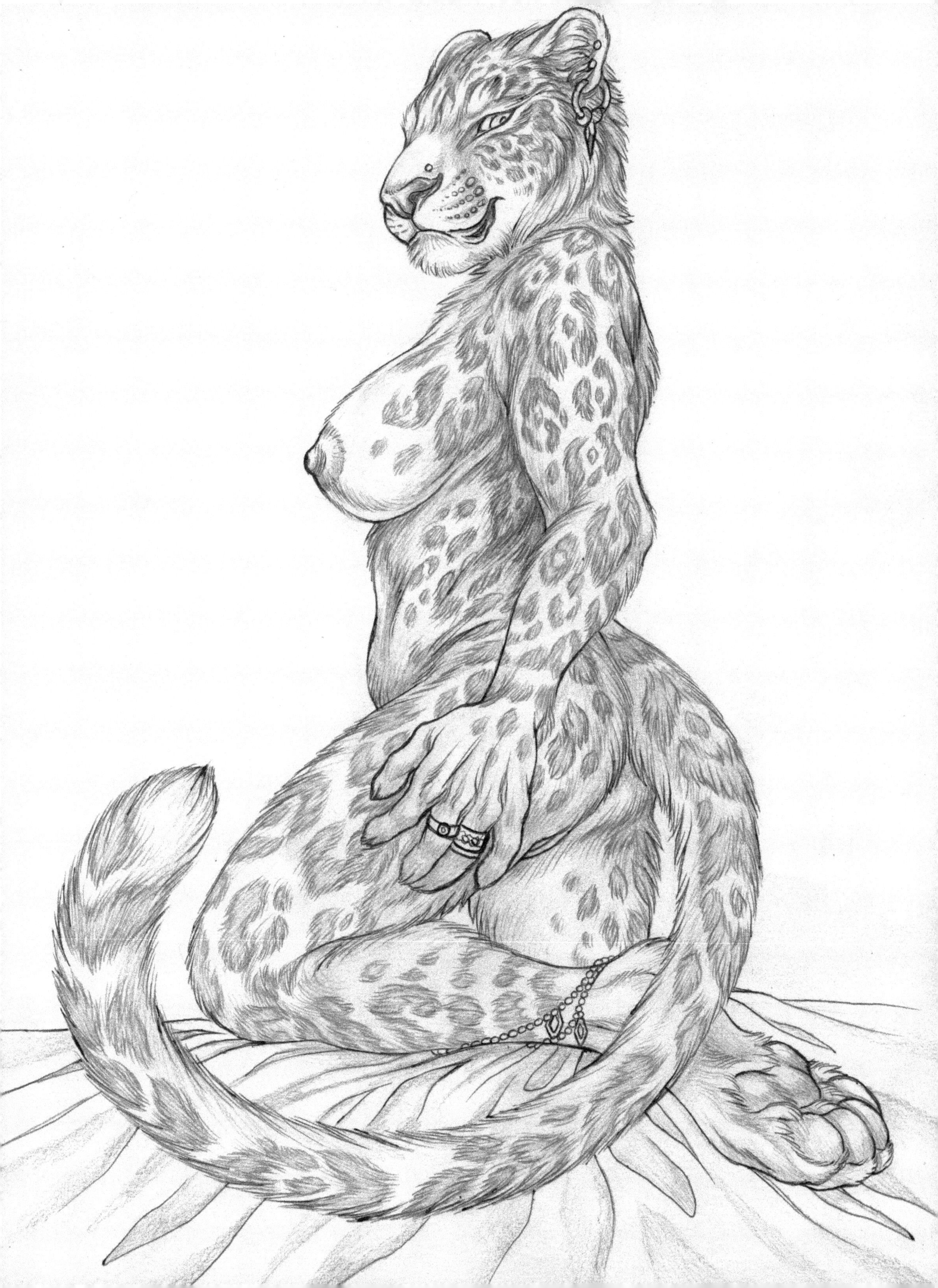

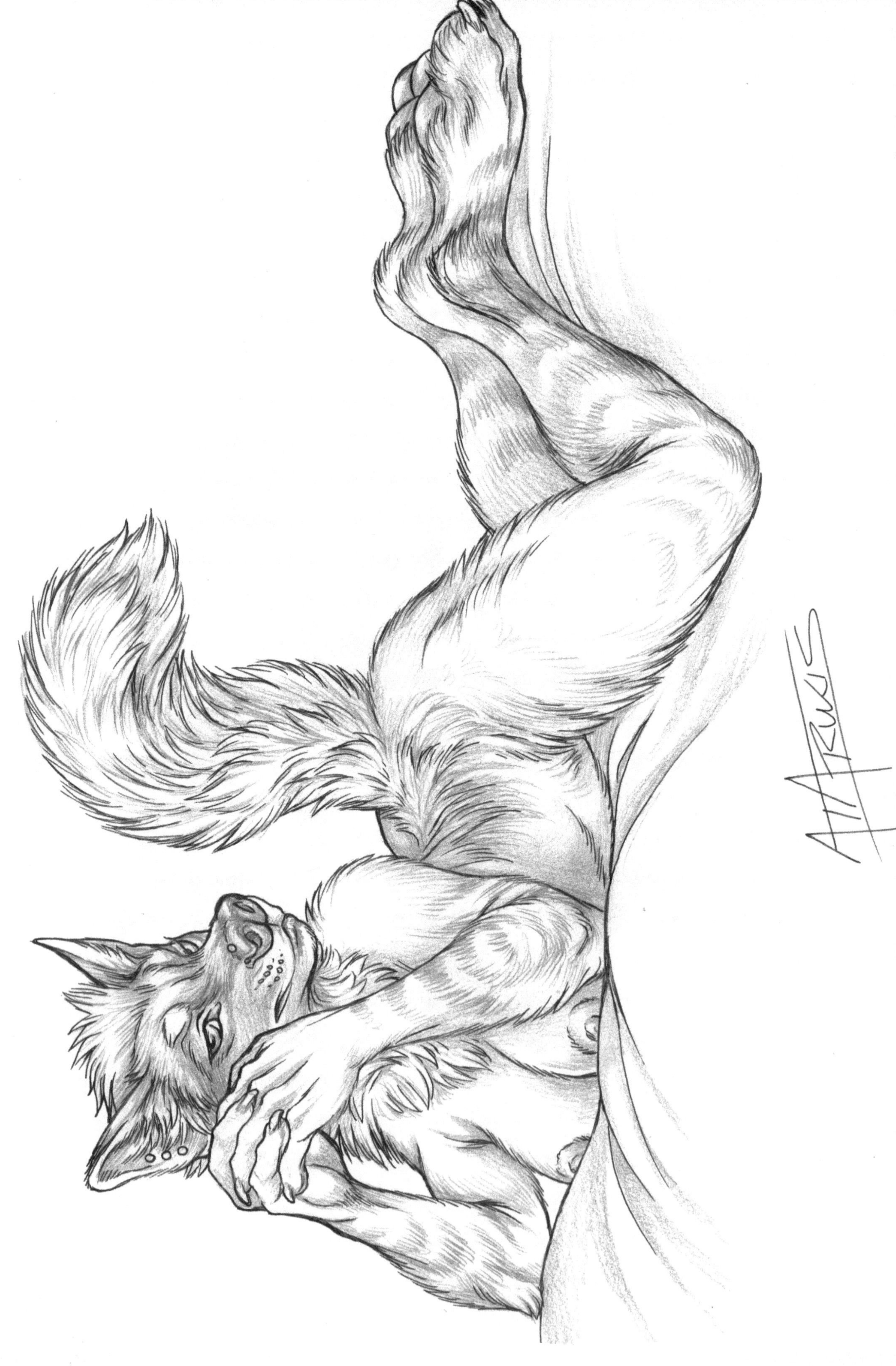

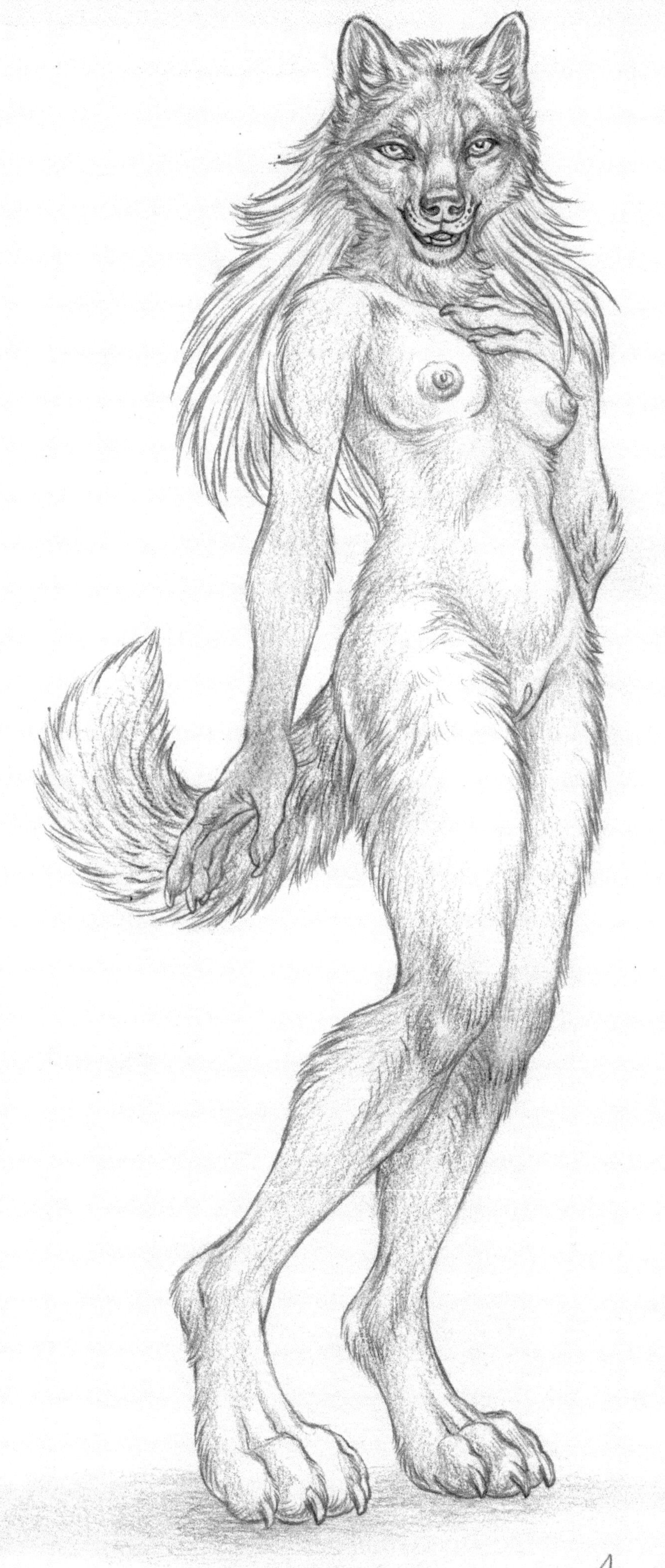

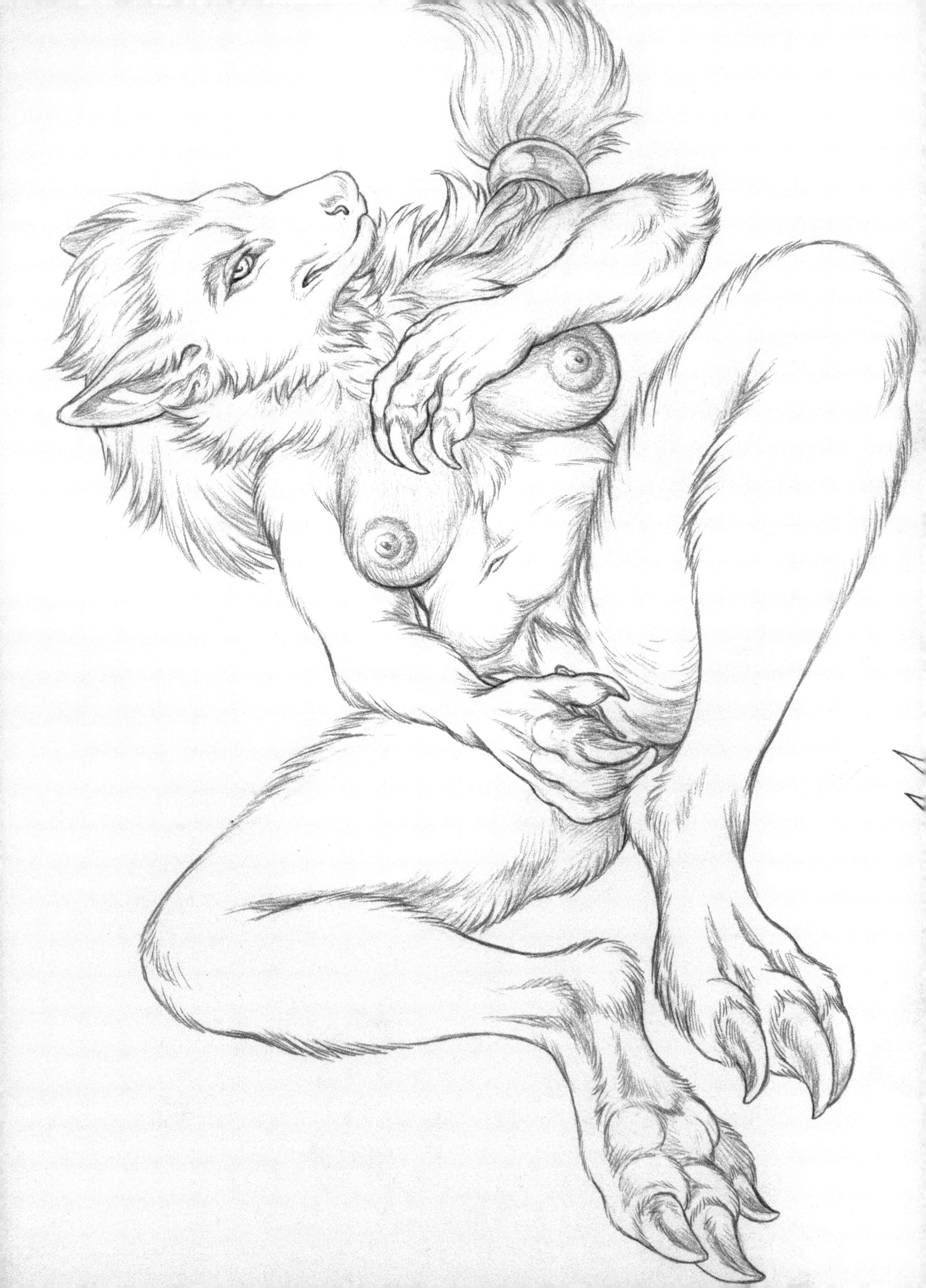

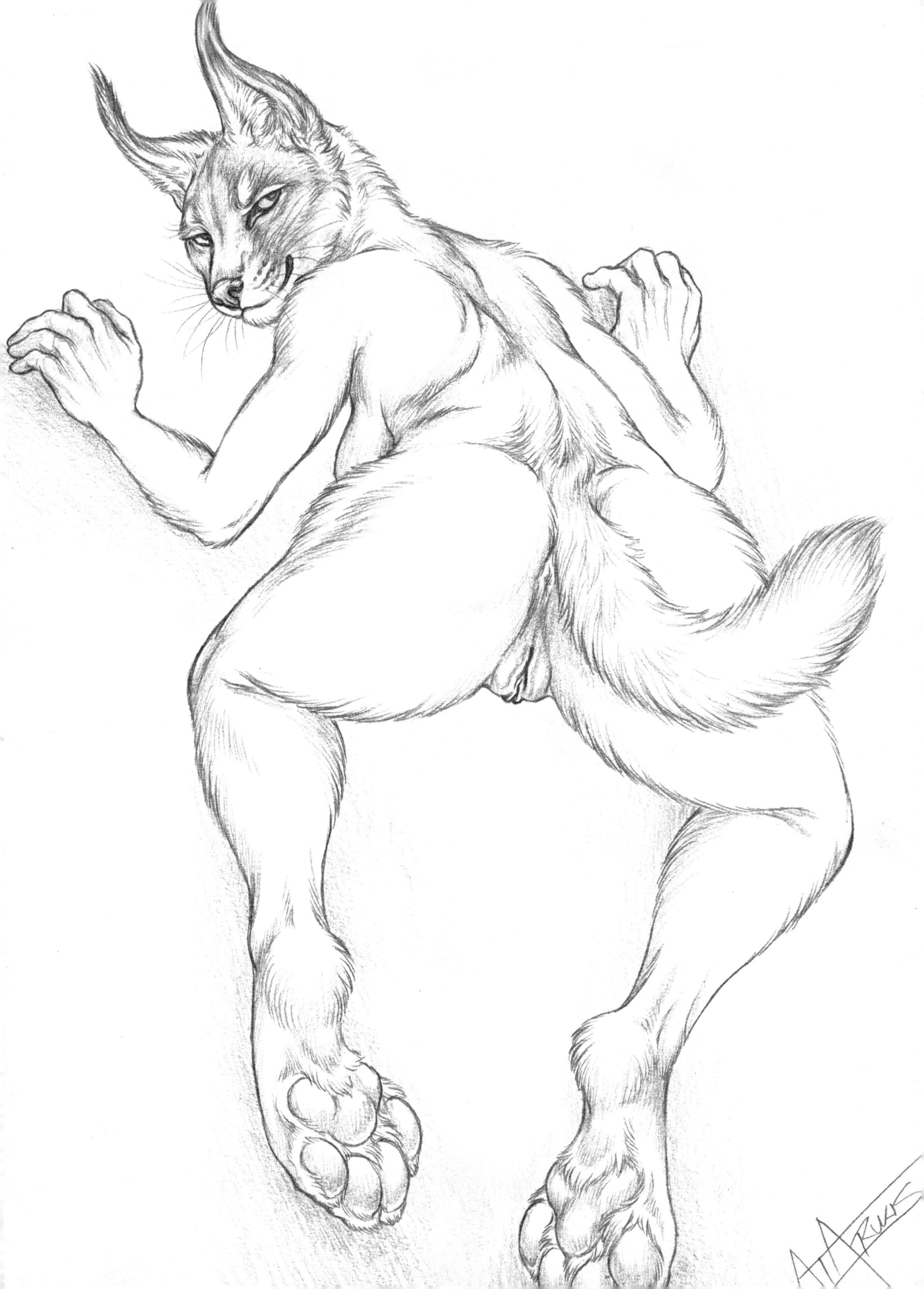

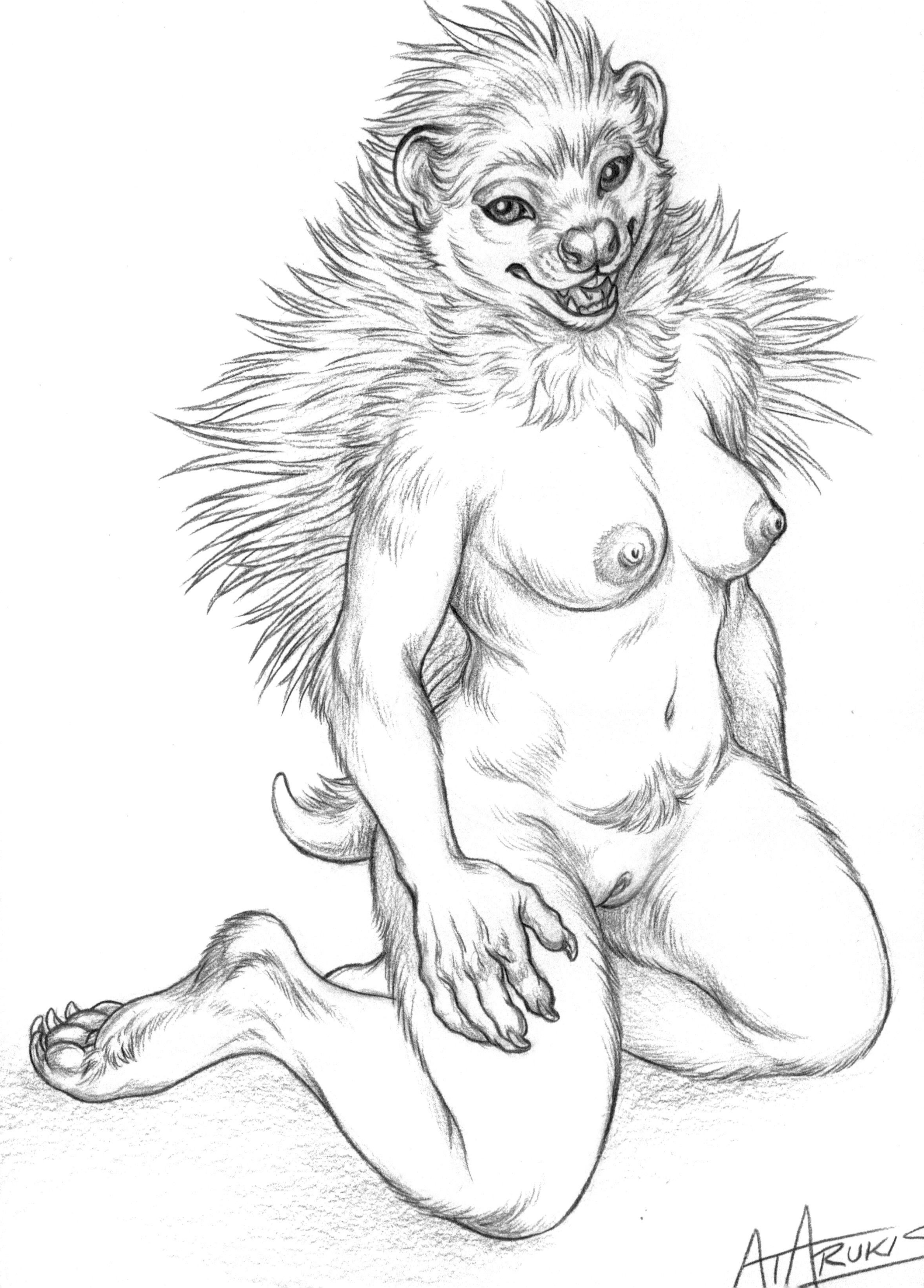

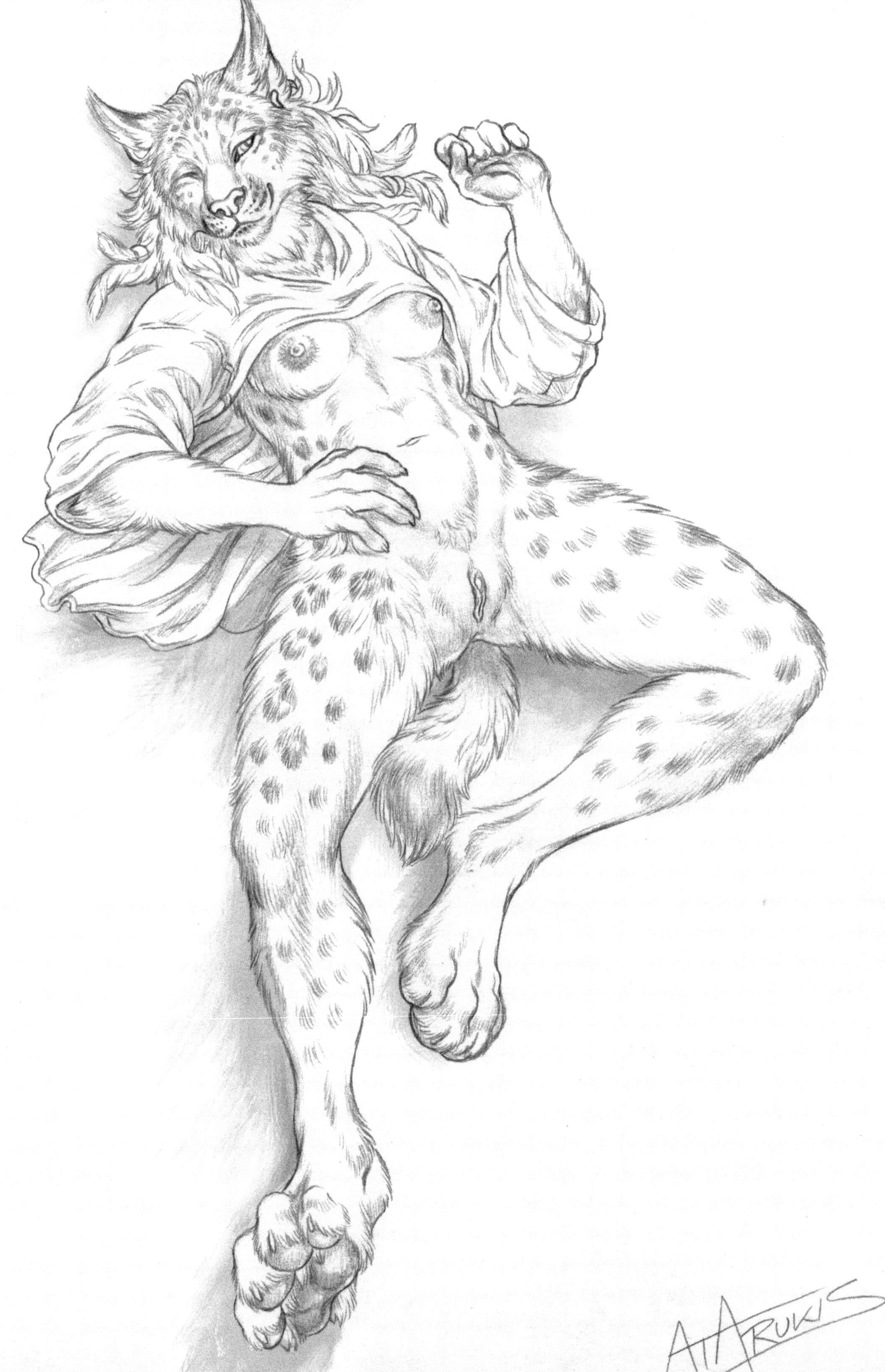

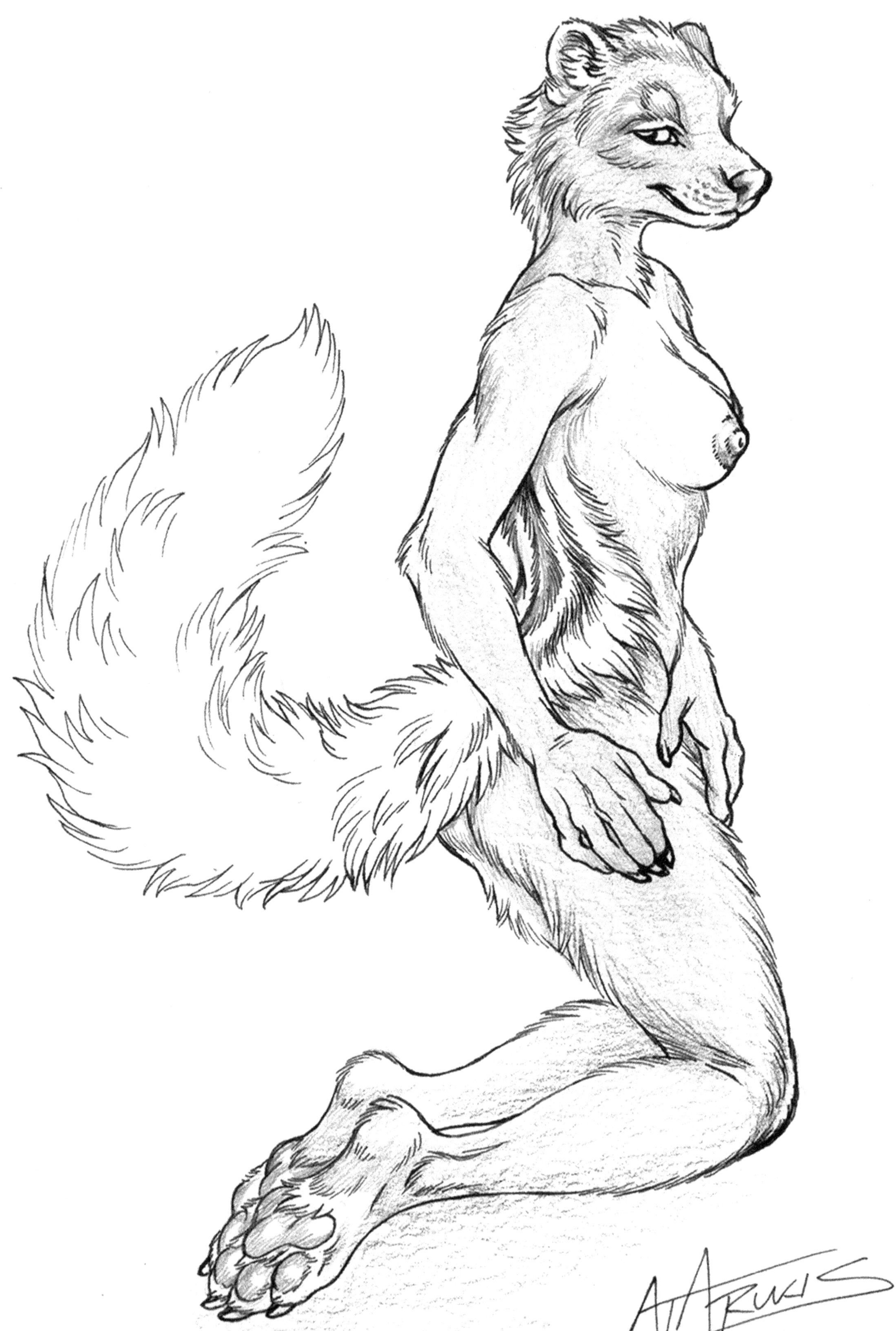

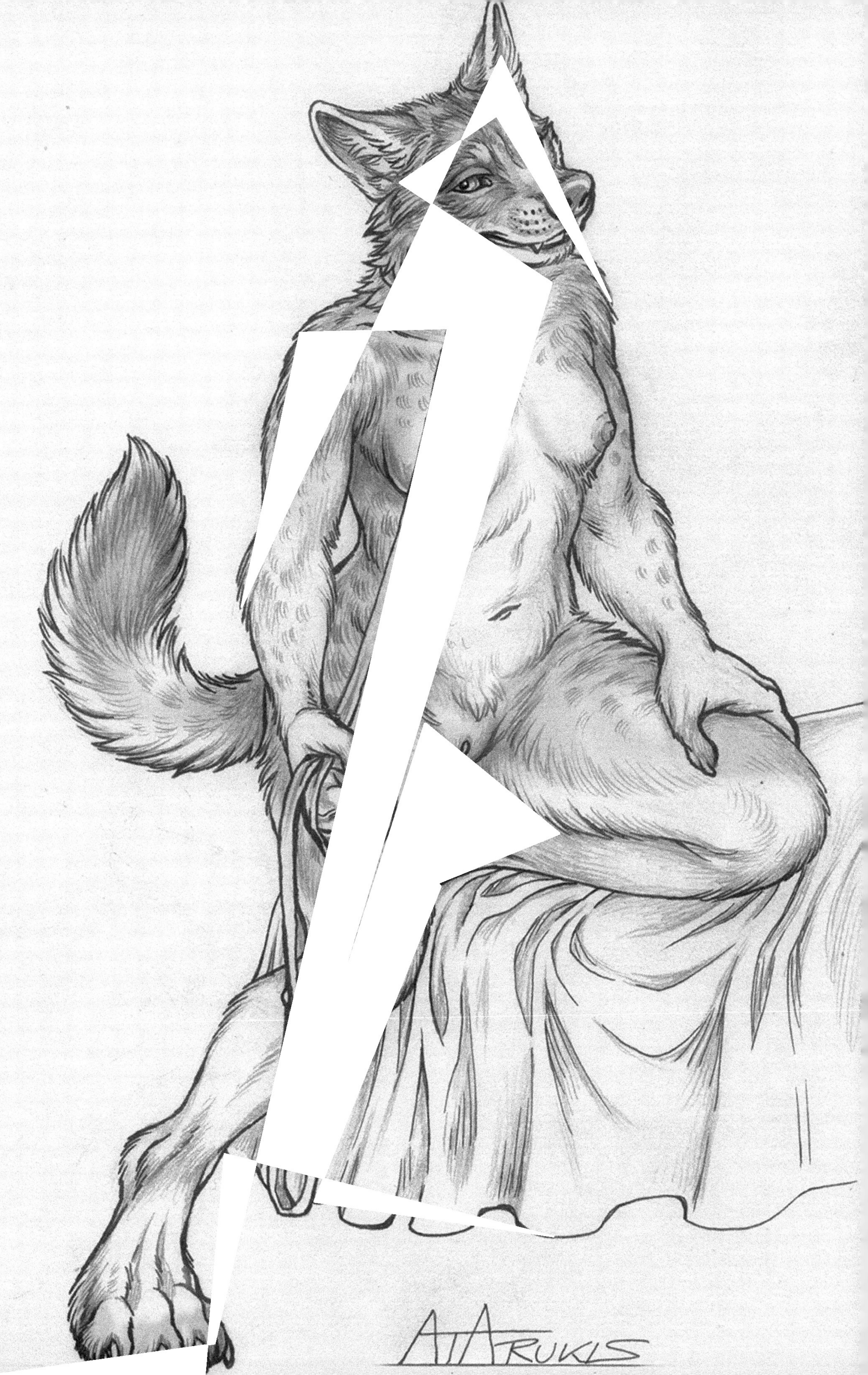

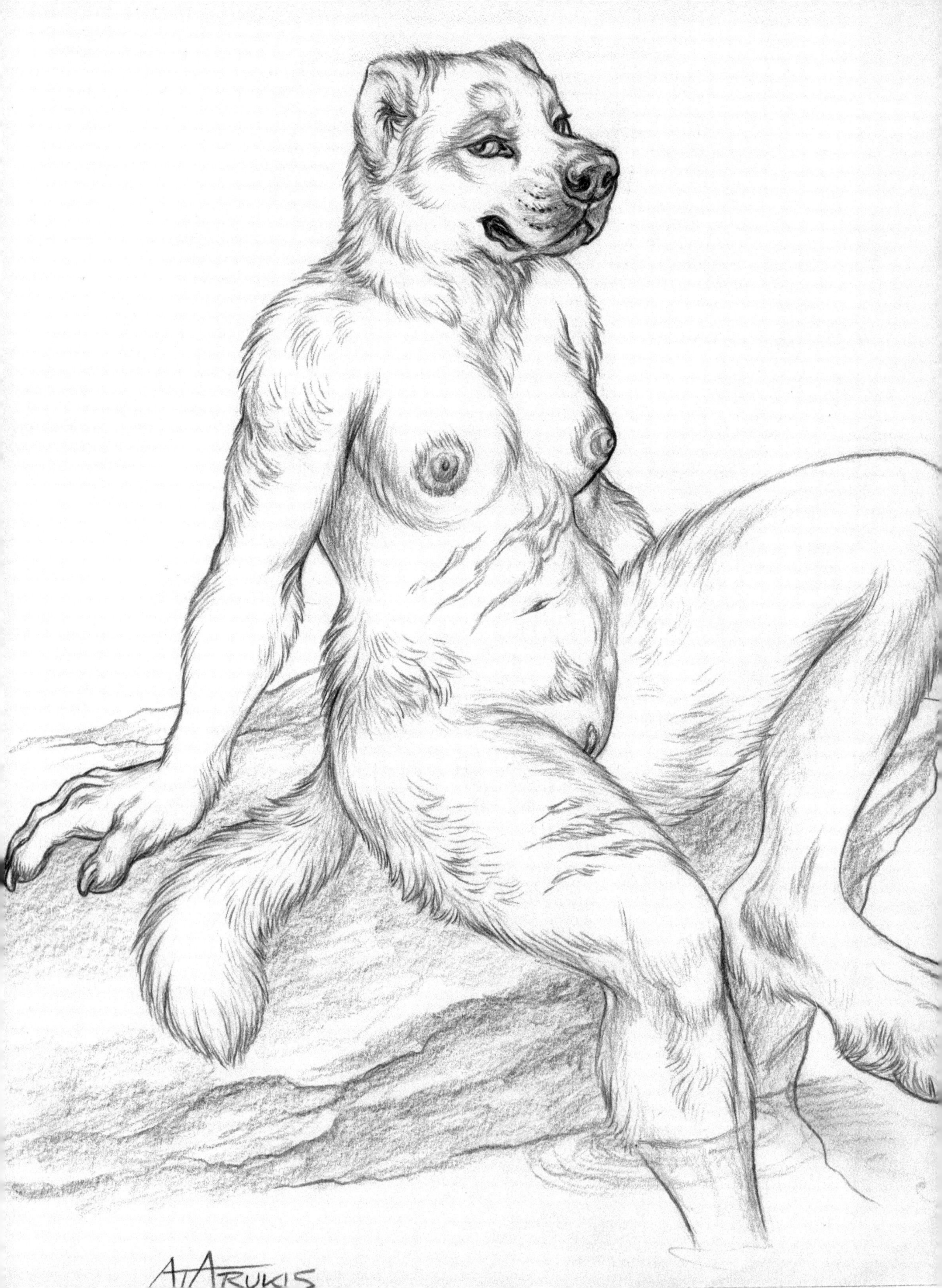

ATARUKIS

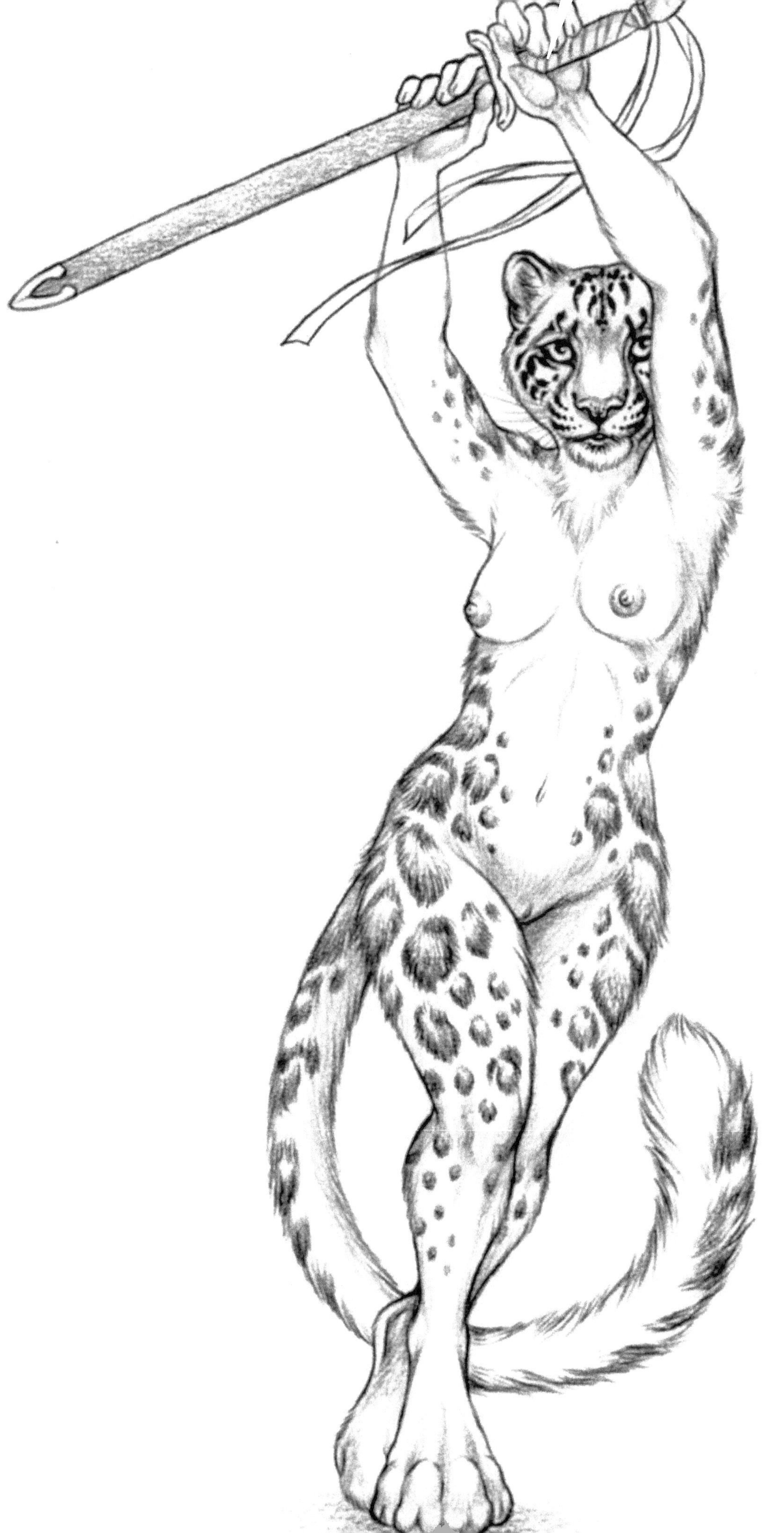

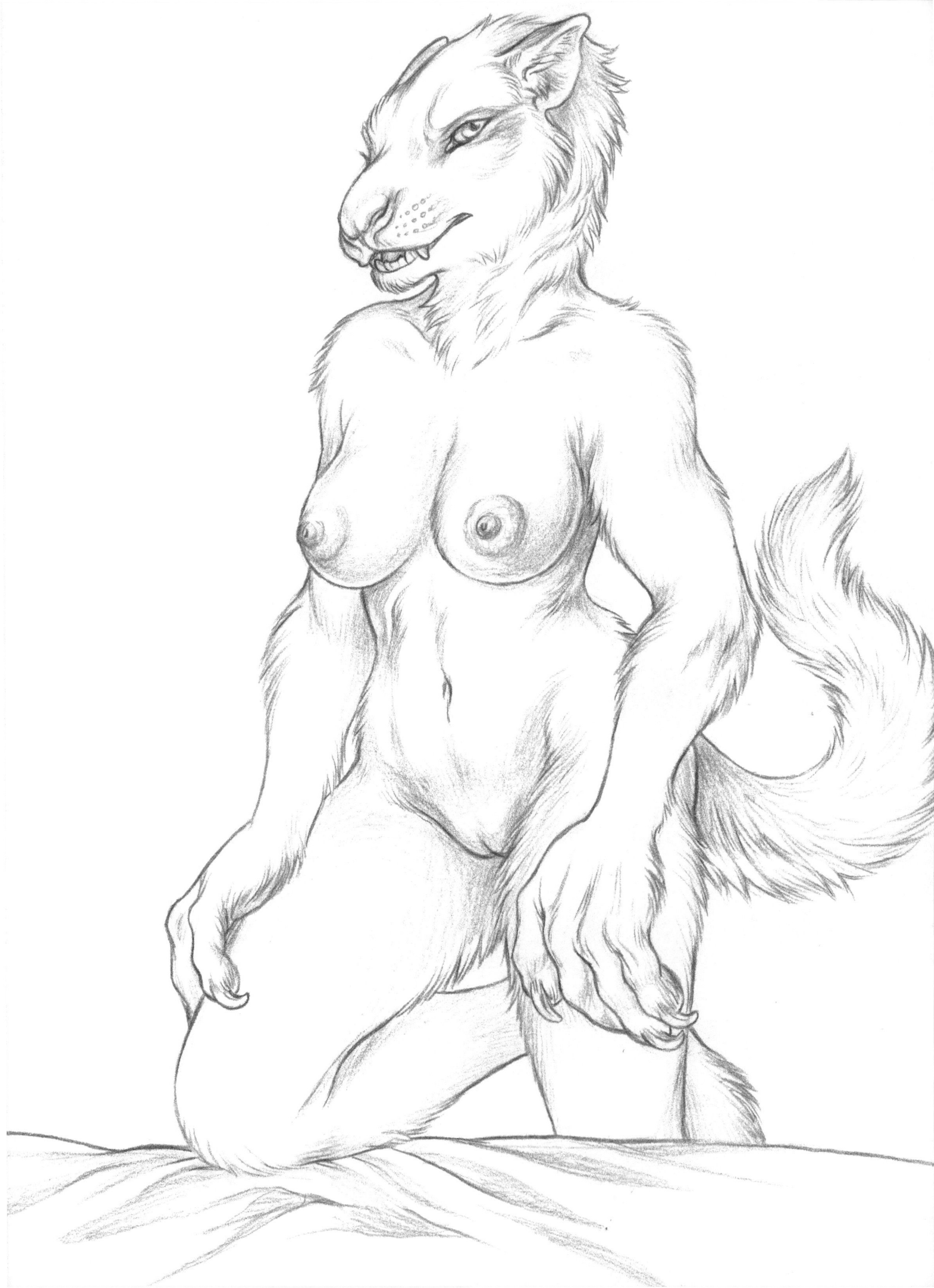

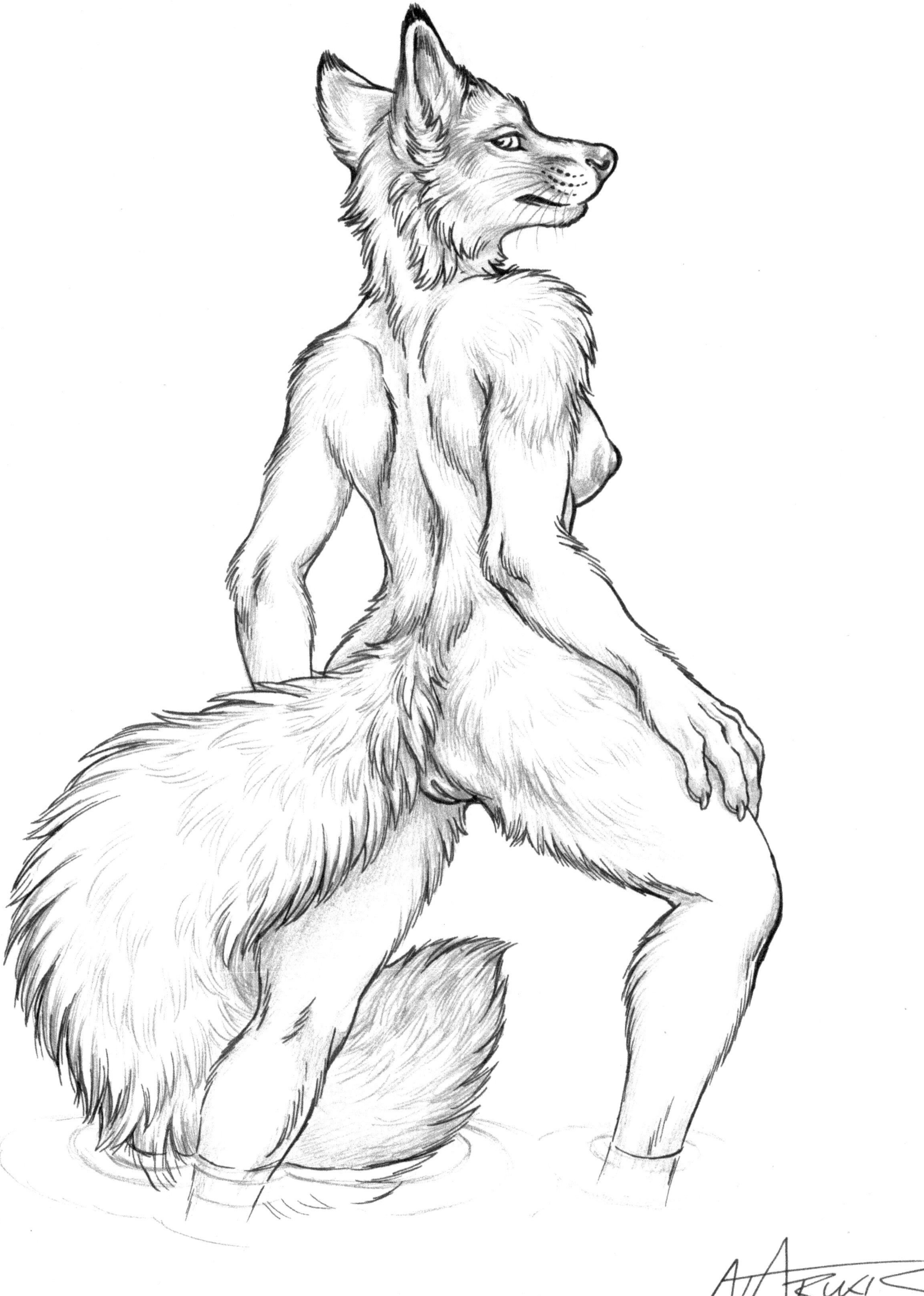

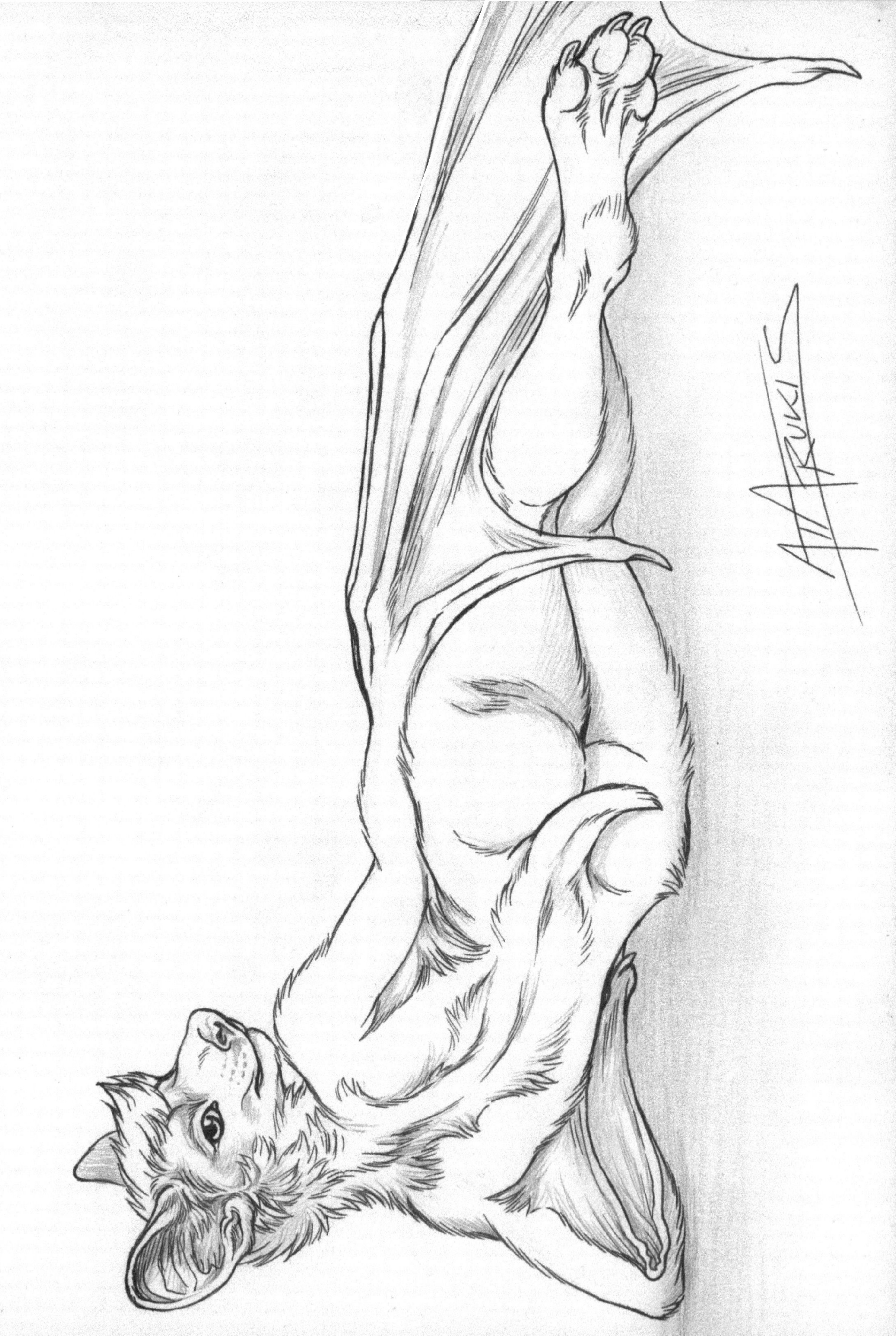

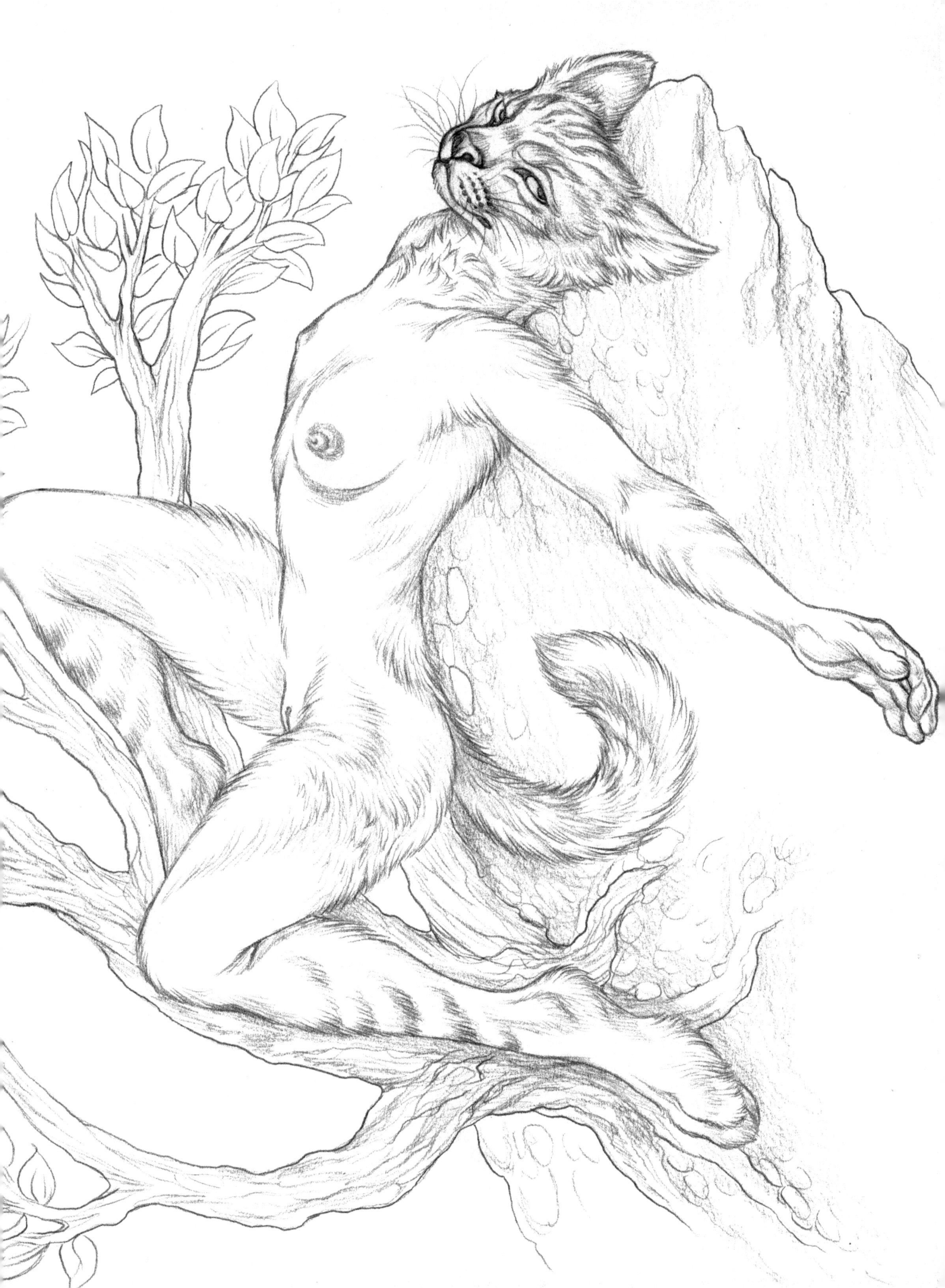

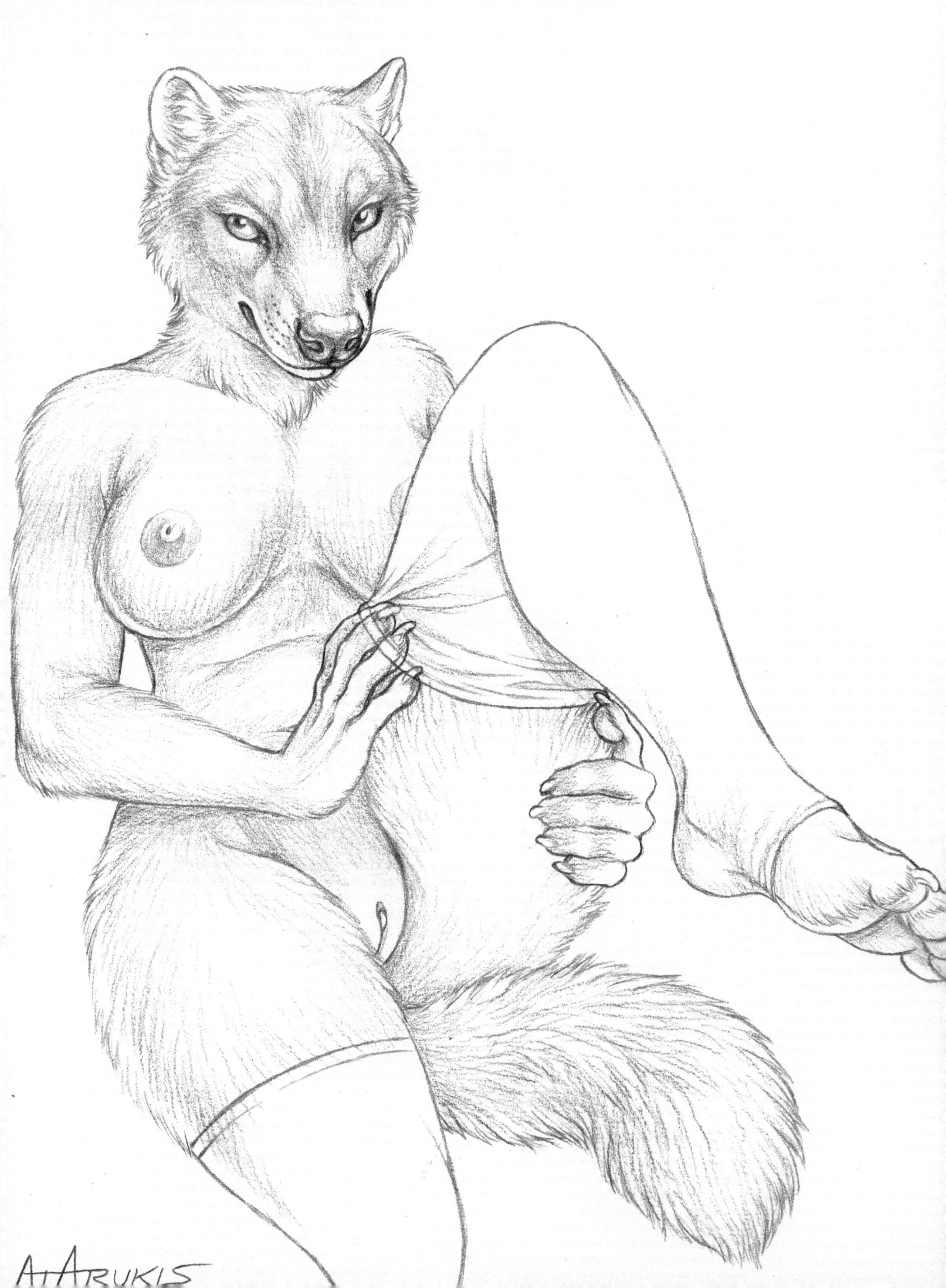

ATARUKIS

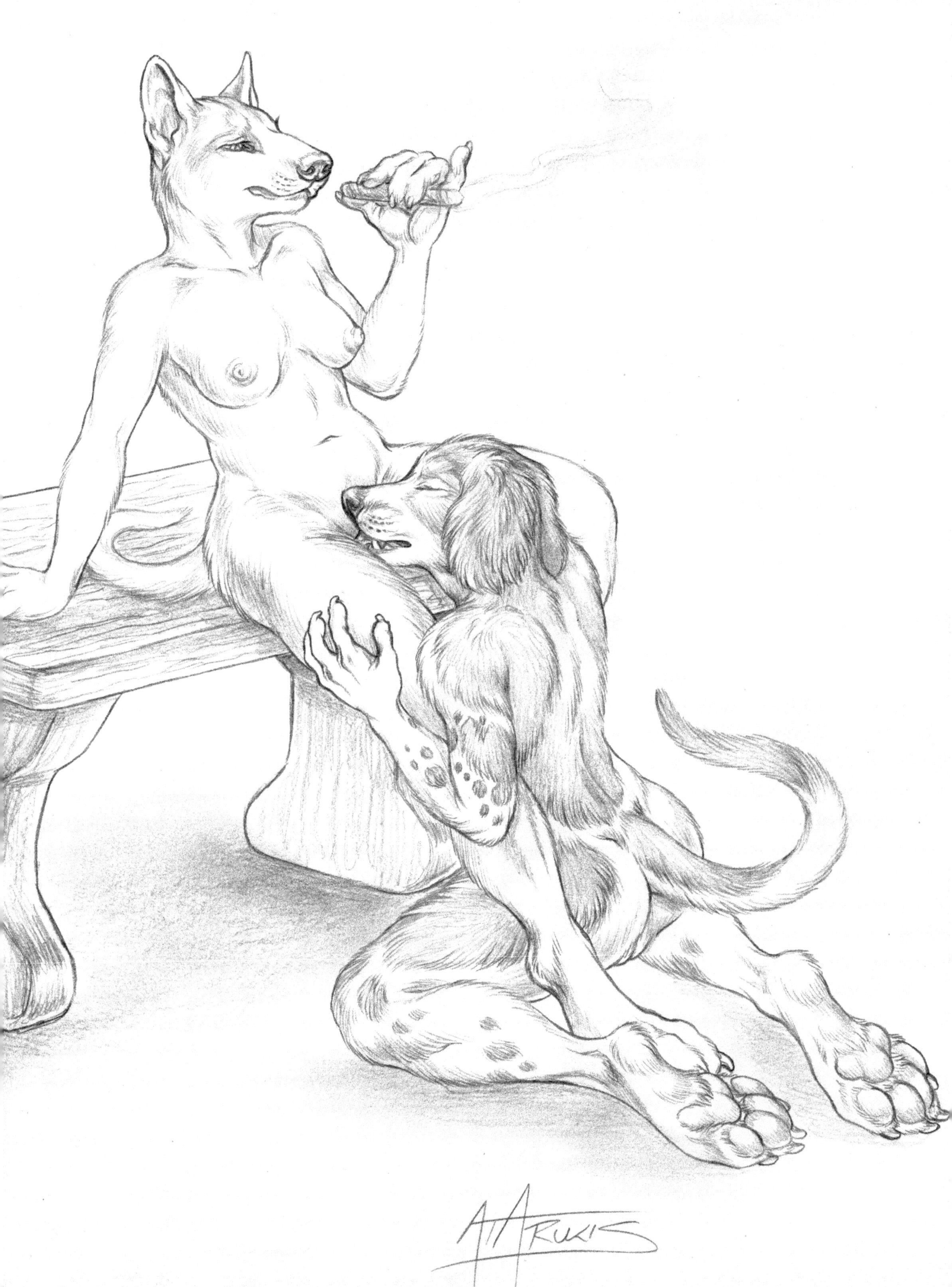

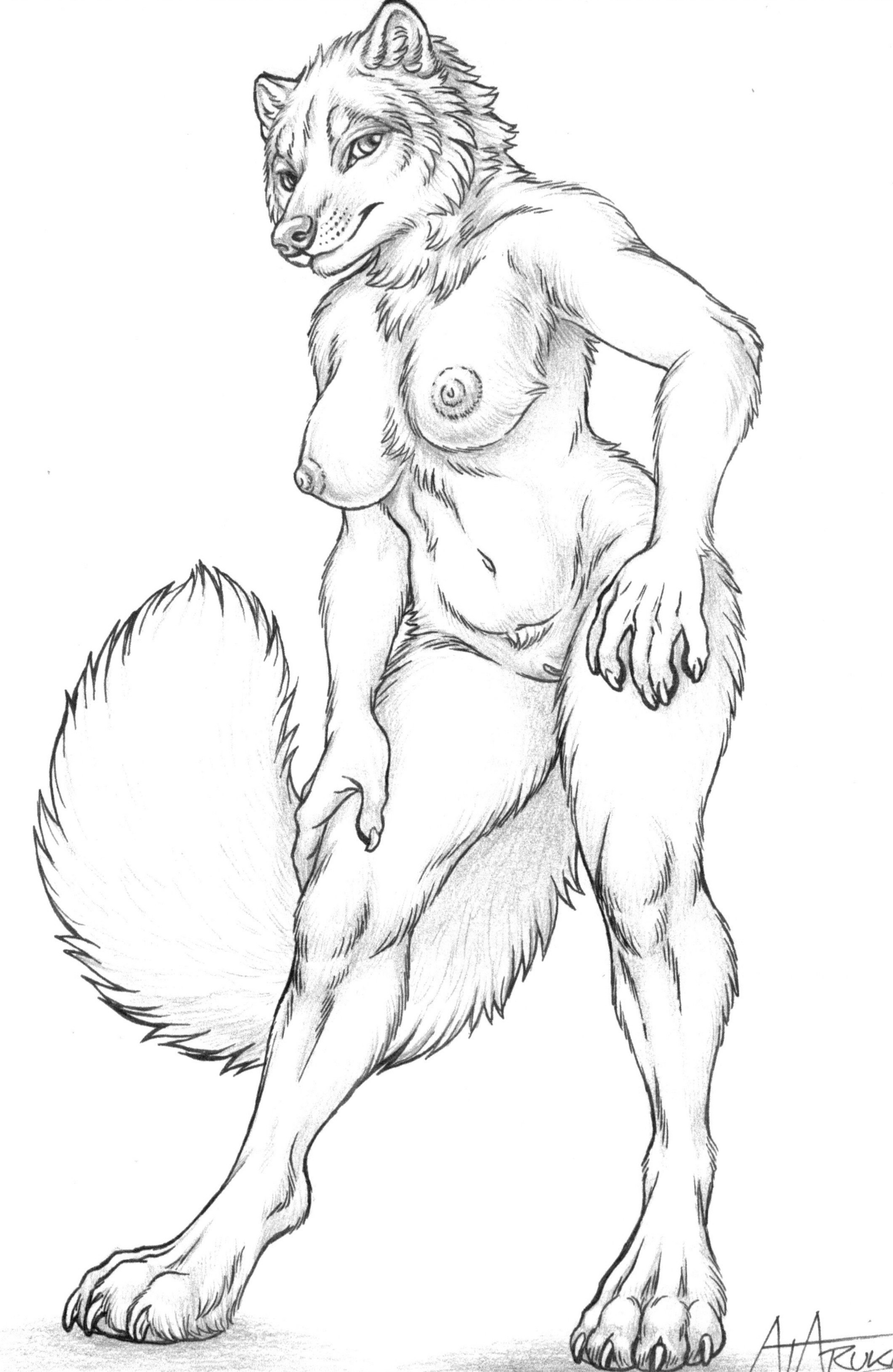

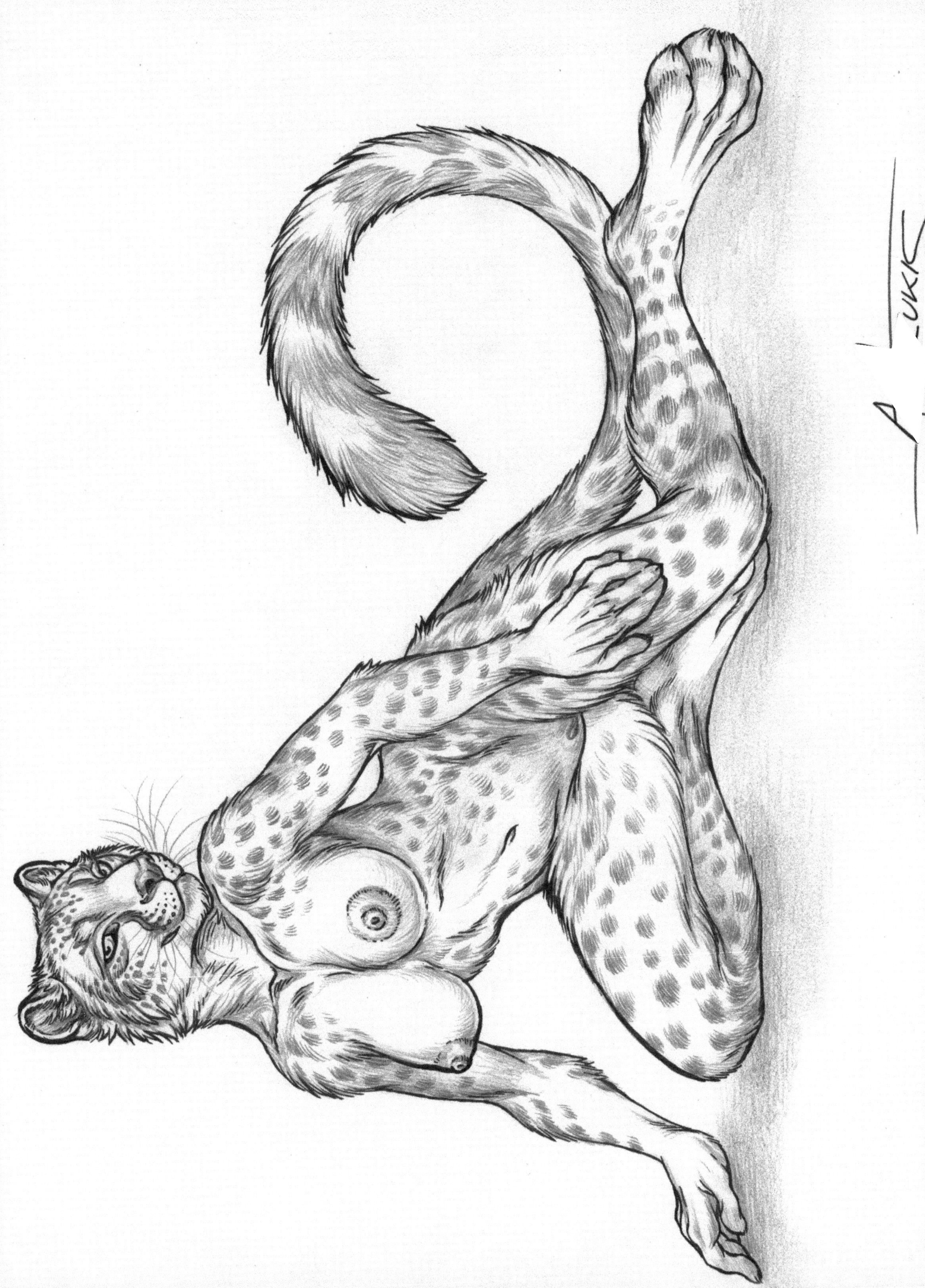

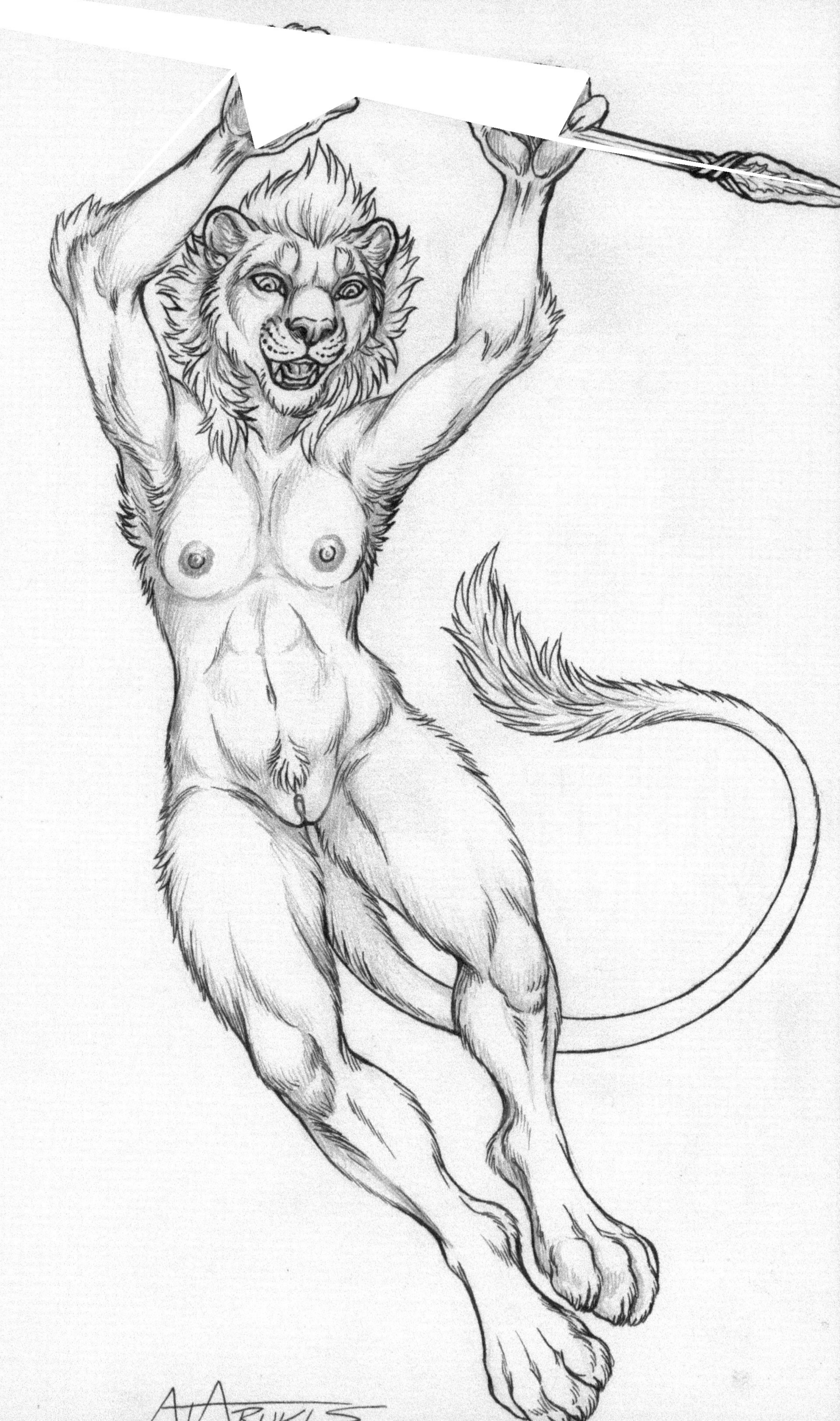

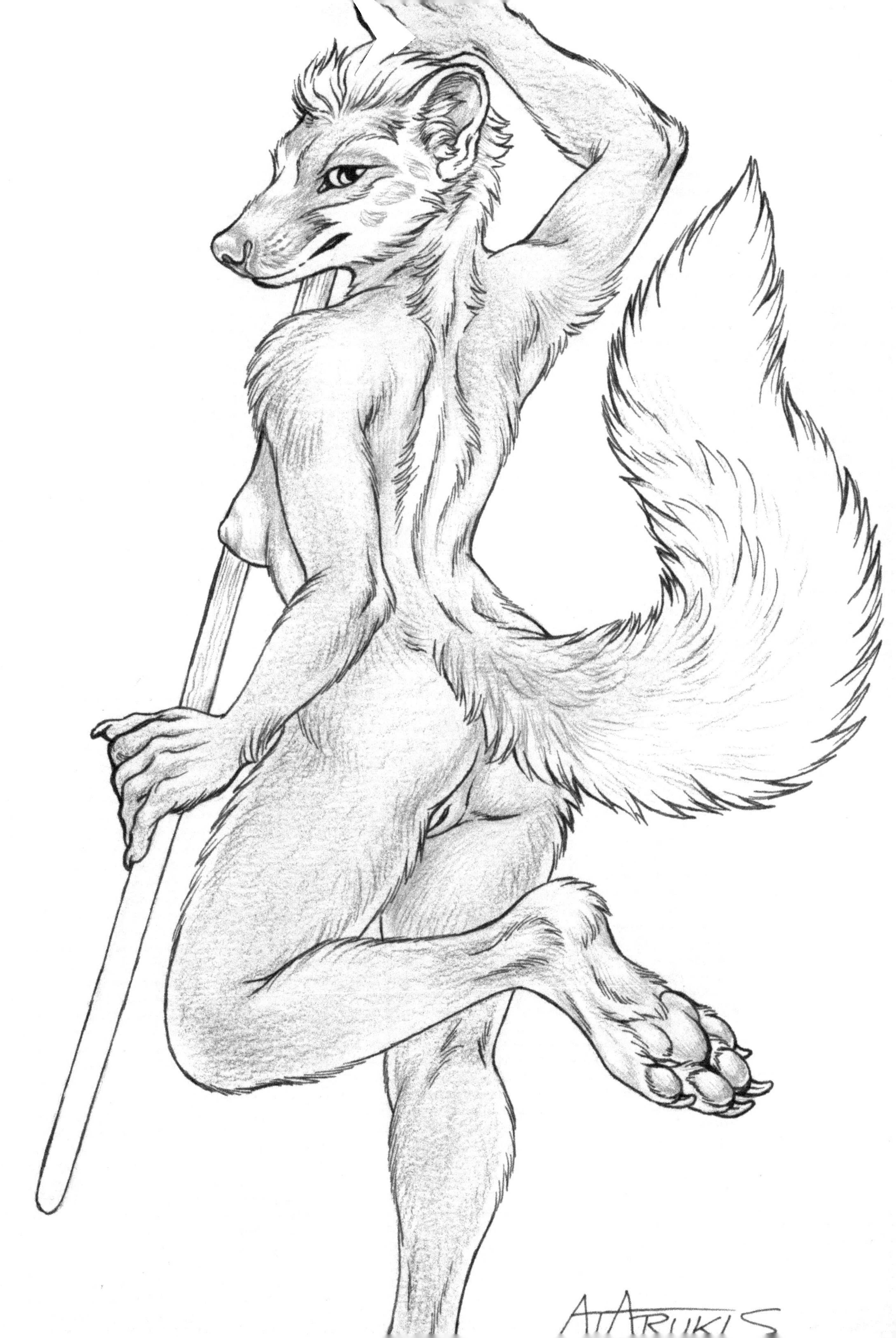

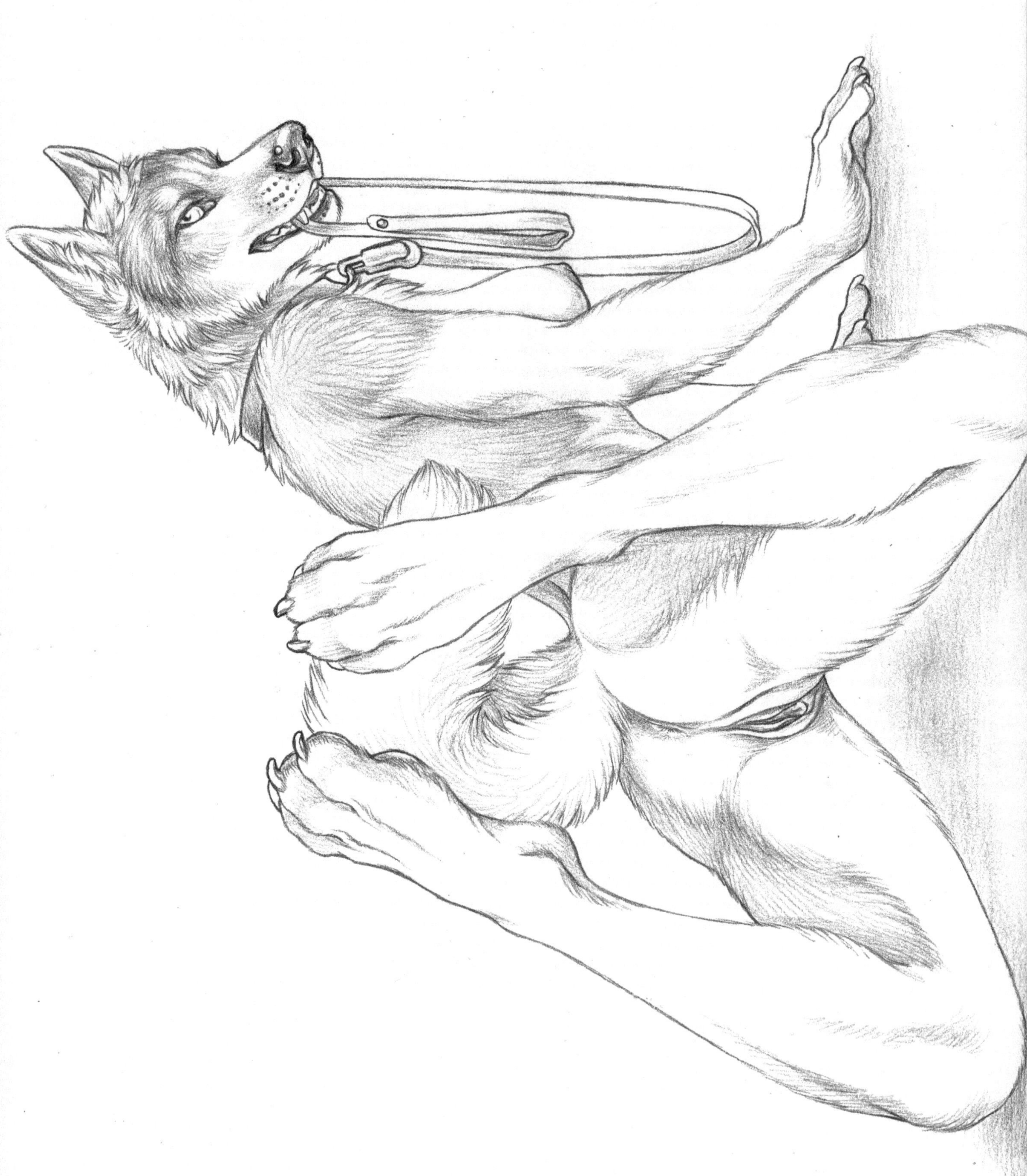

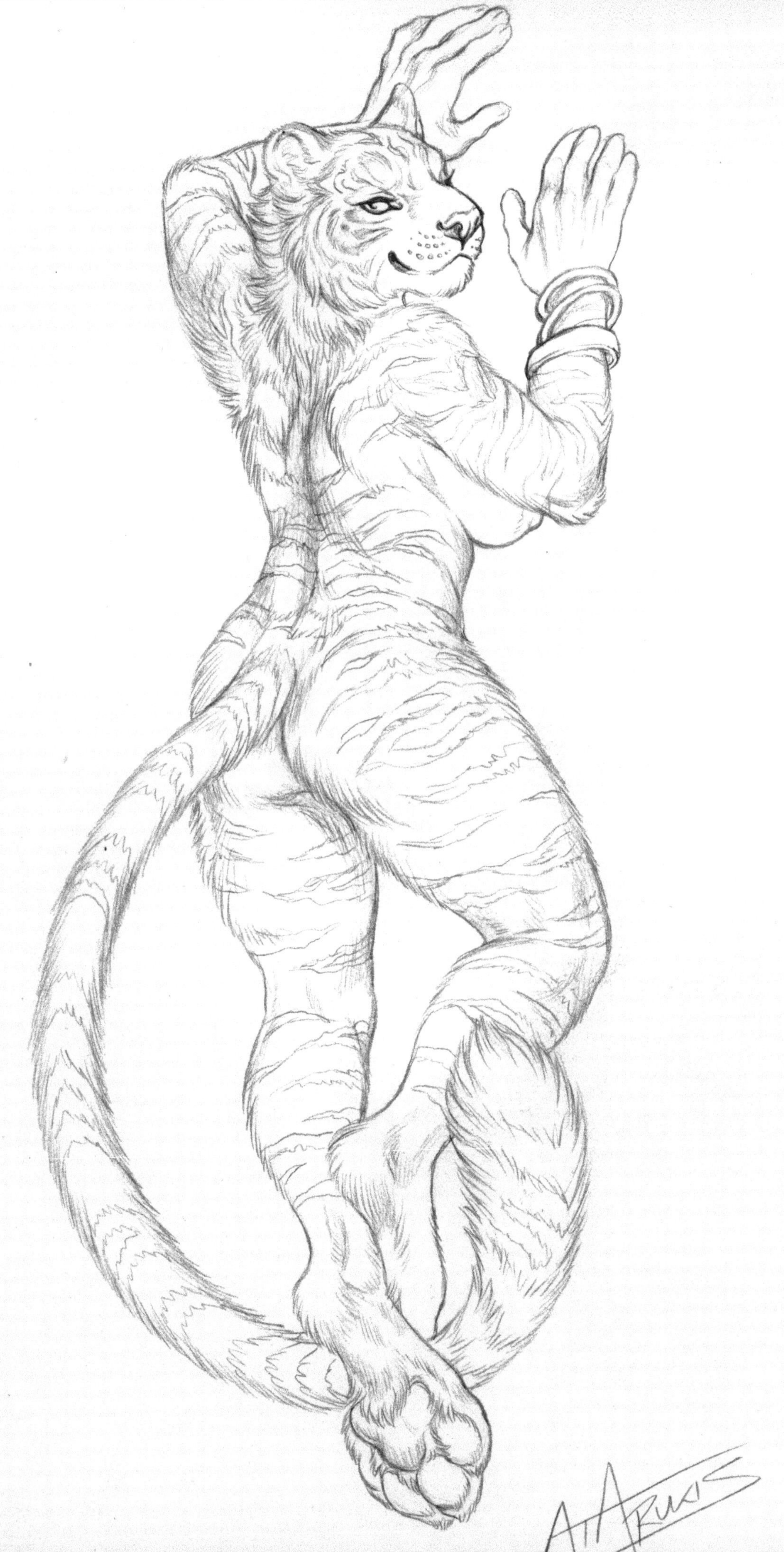

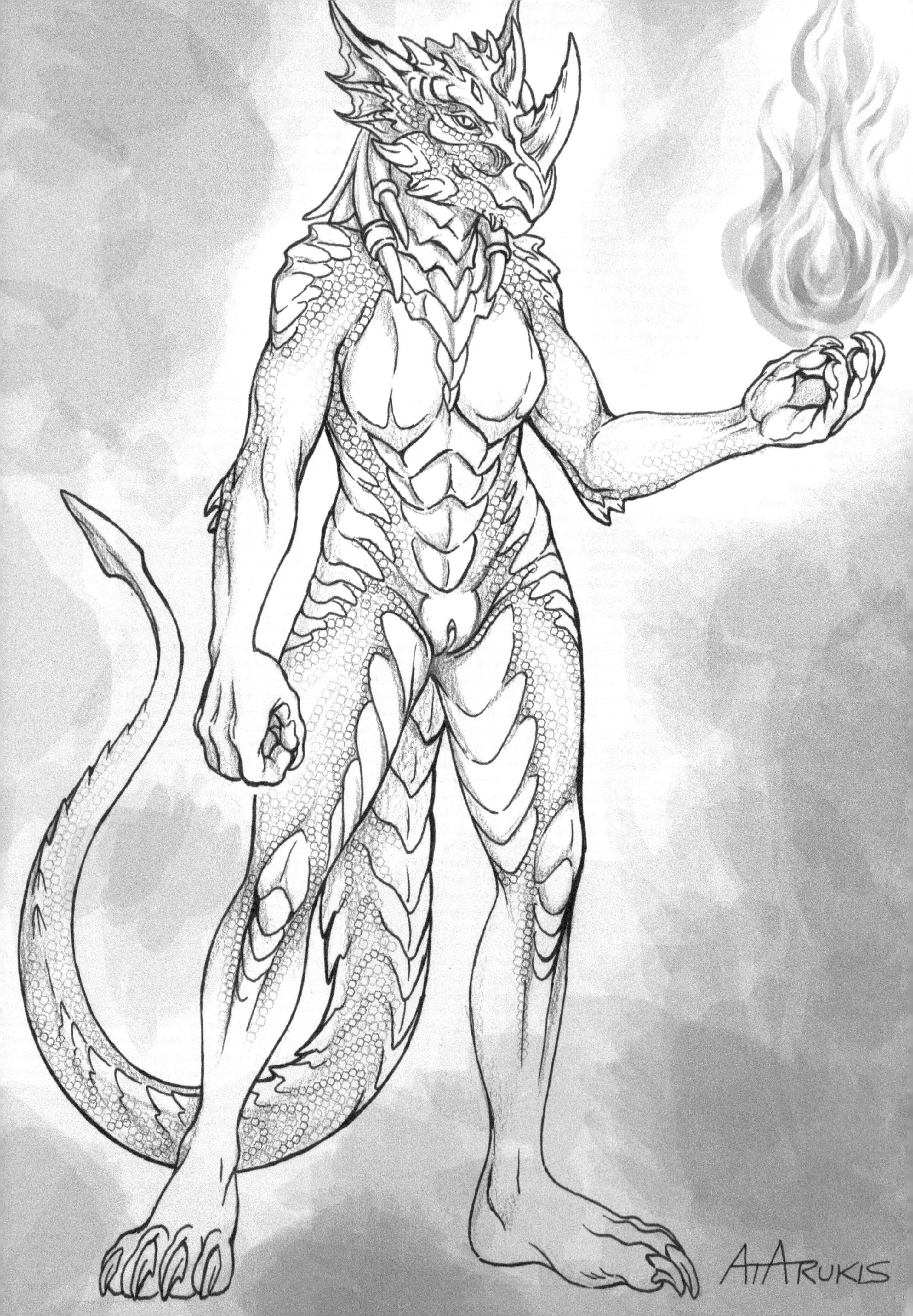

AtArukis

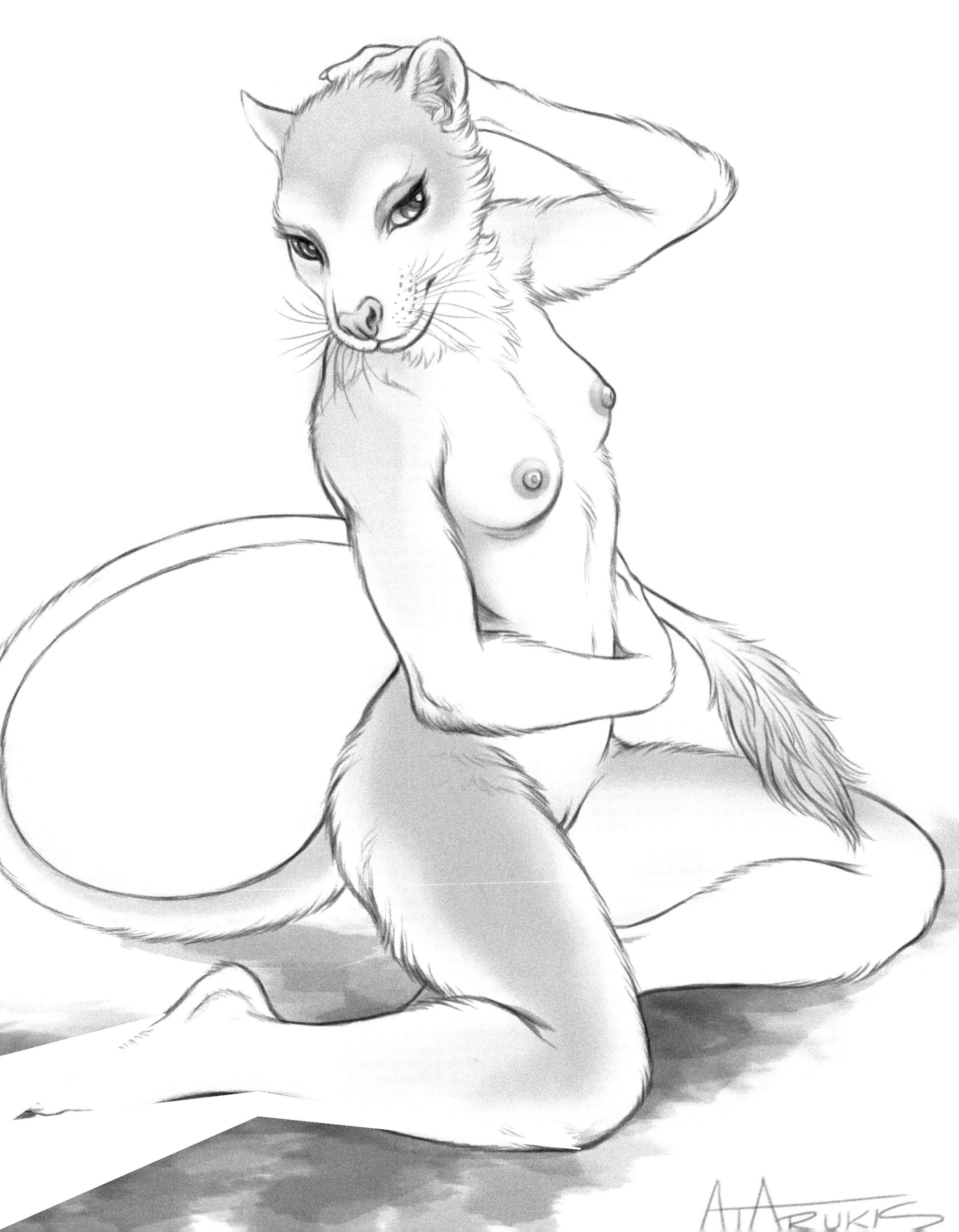

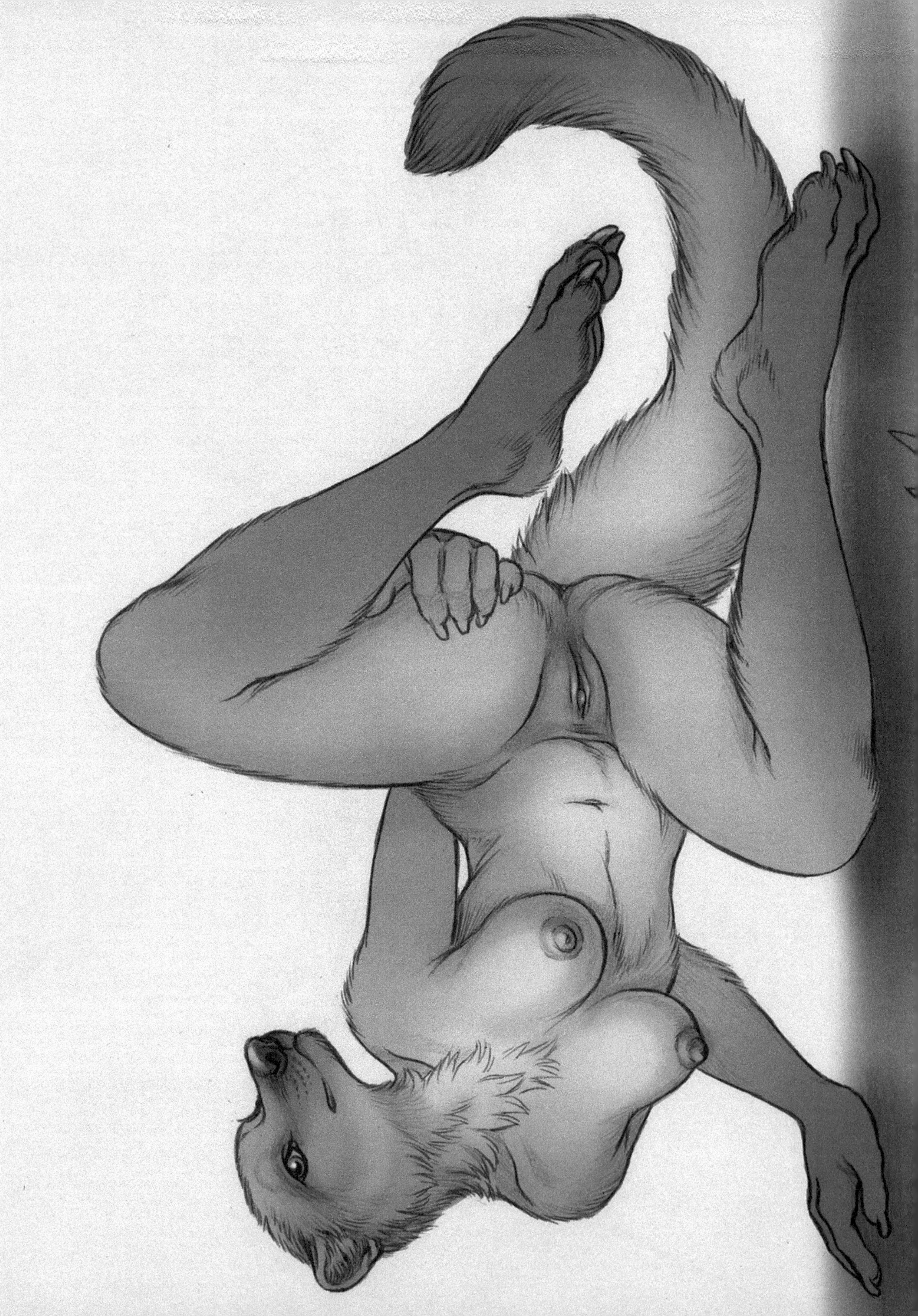

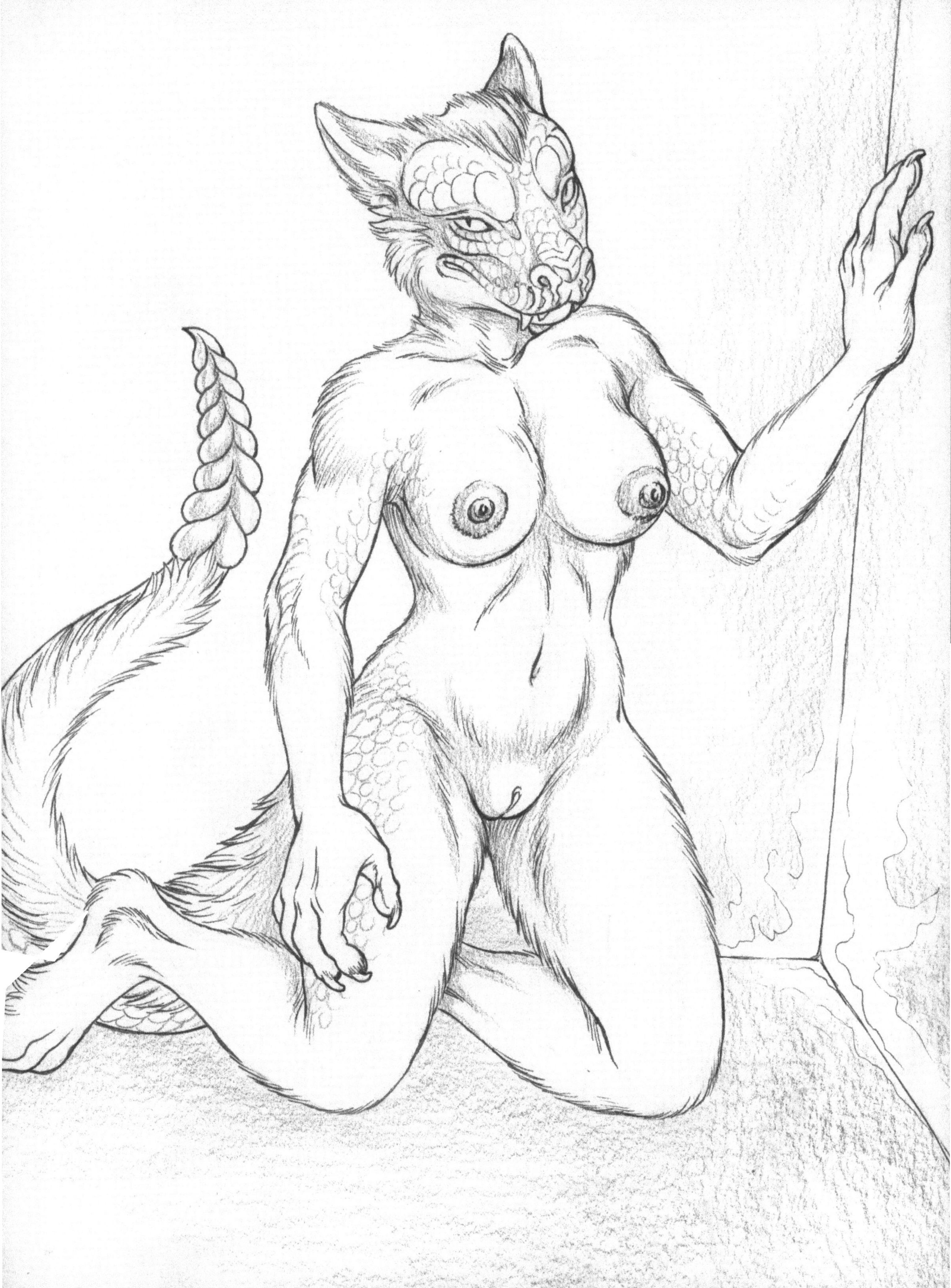

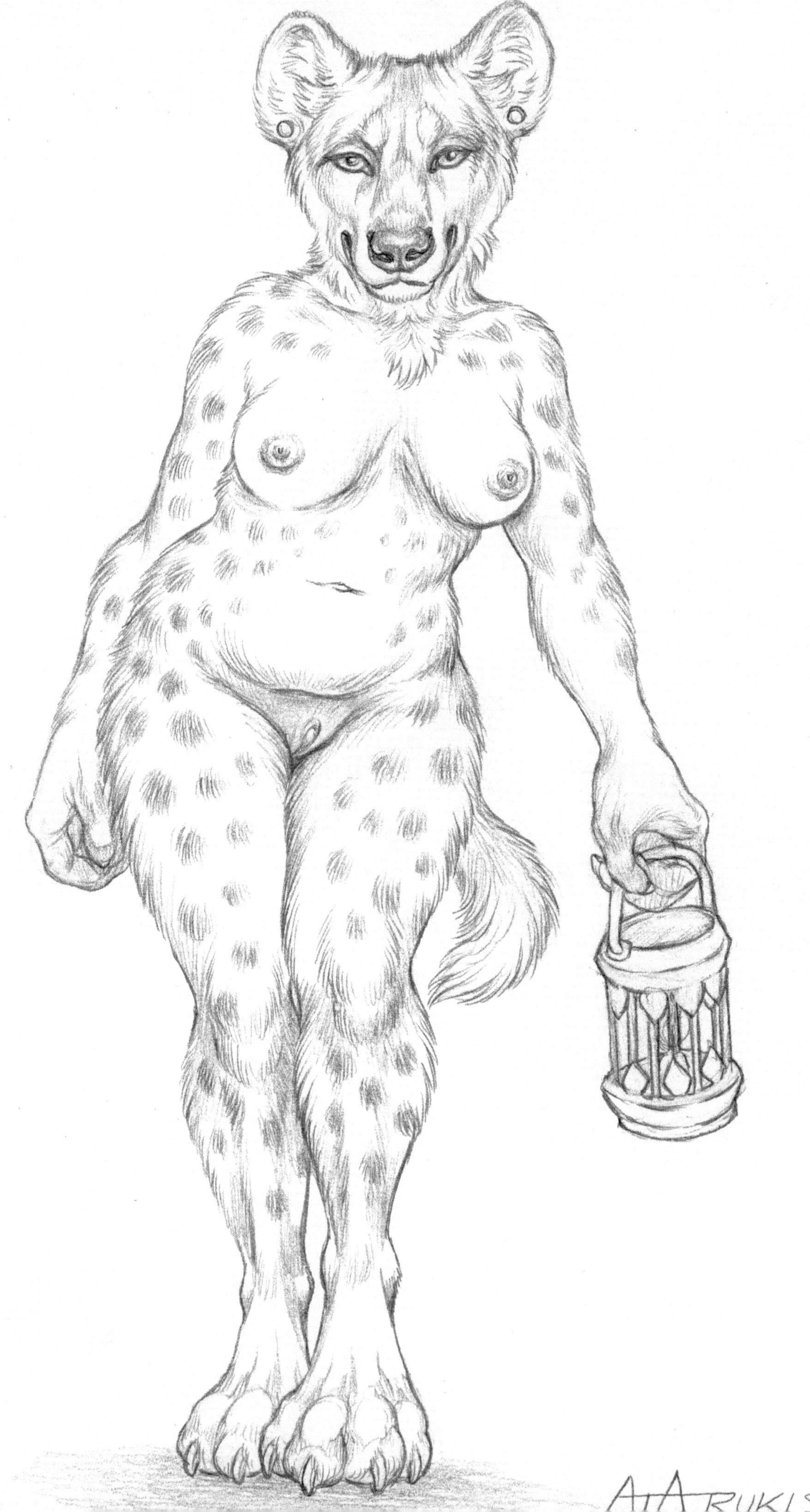

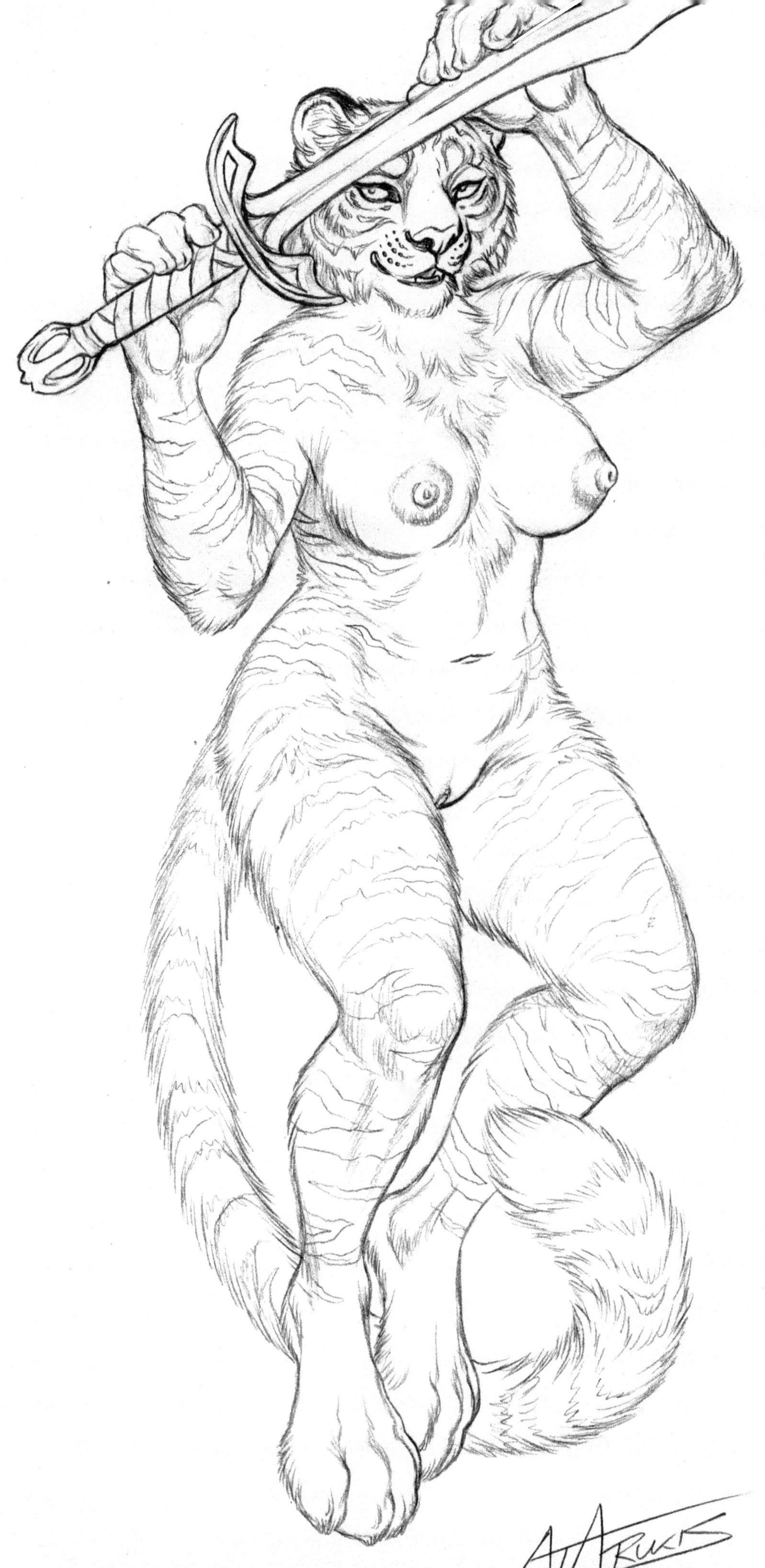

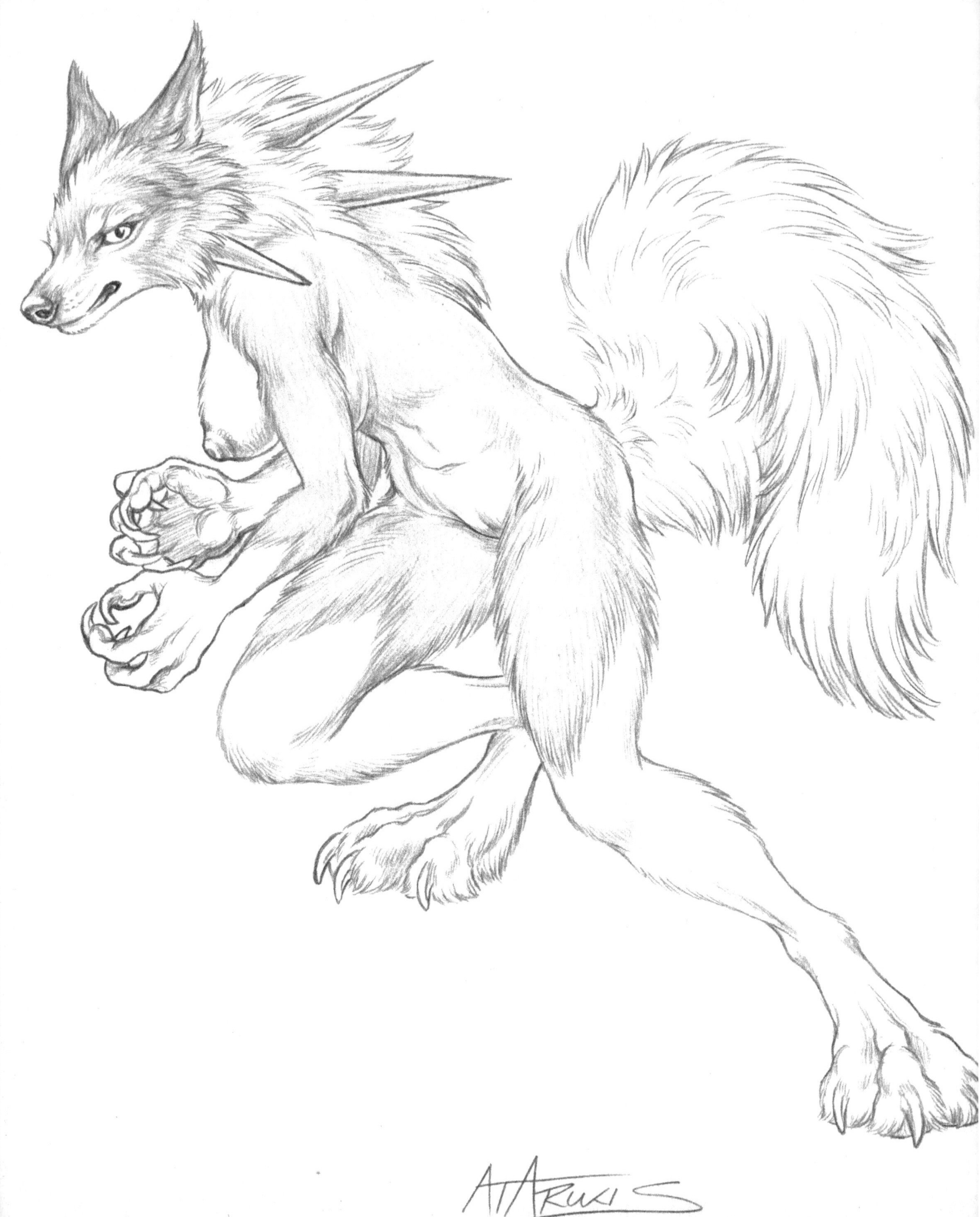

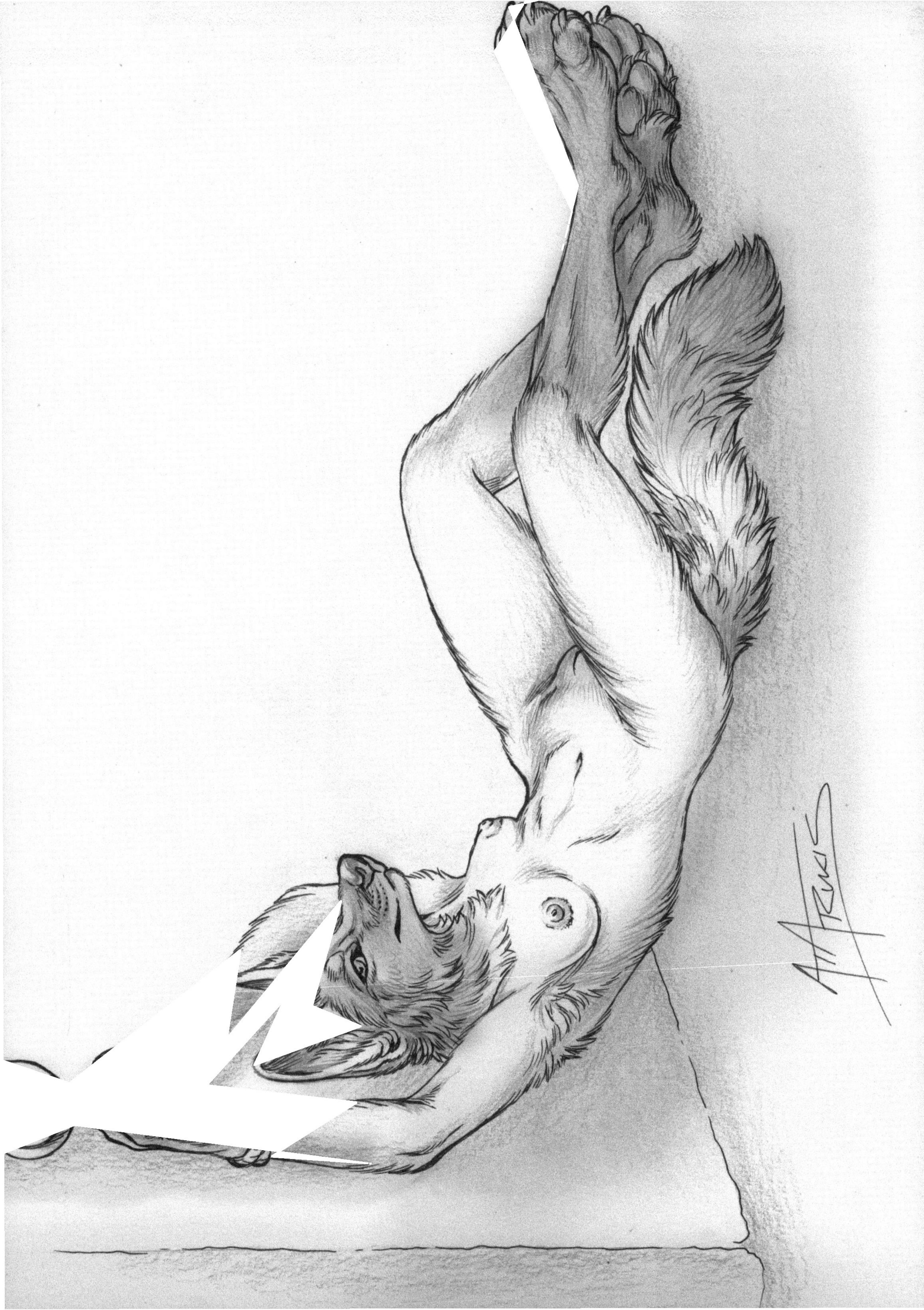

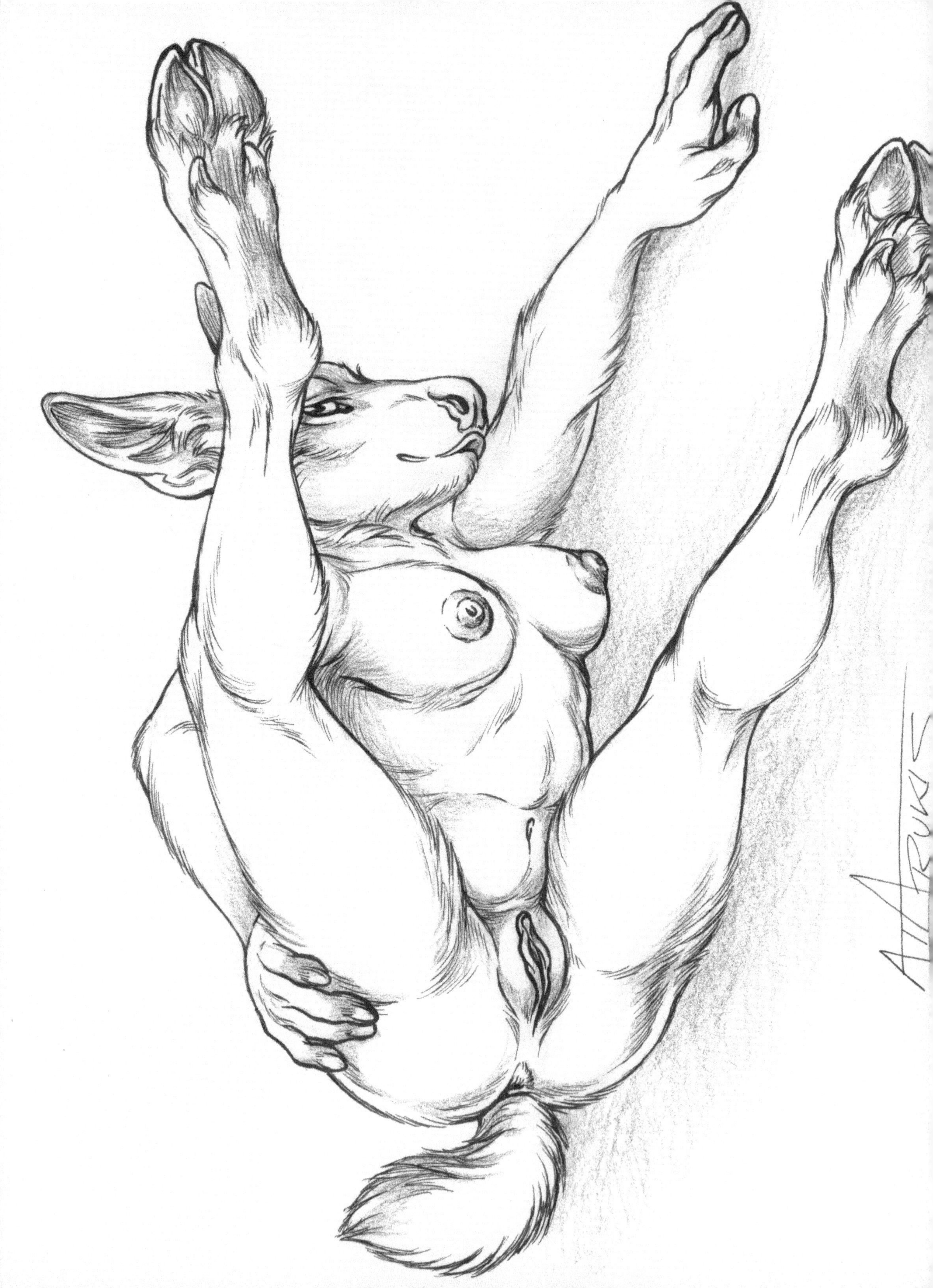

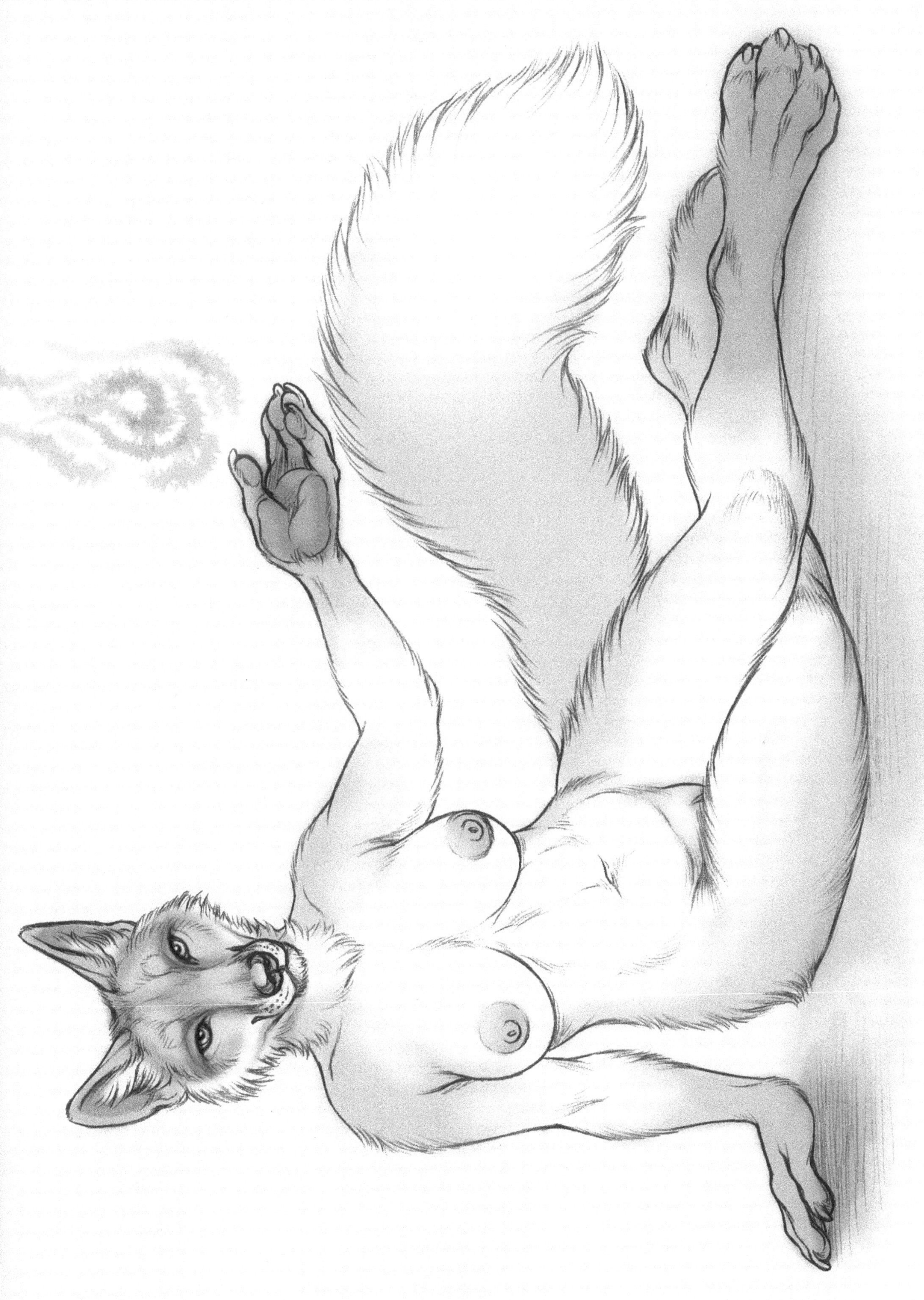

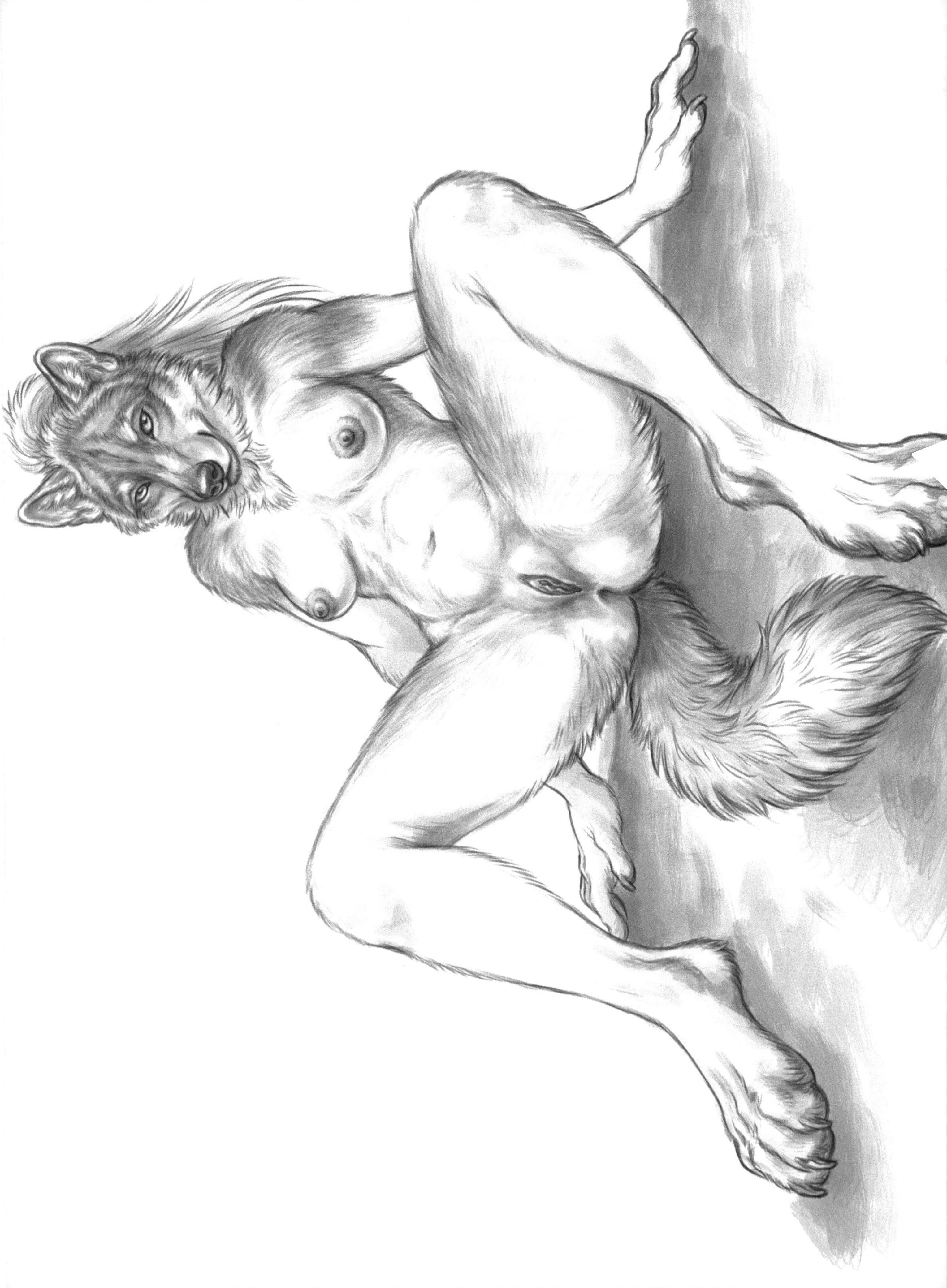

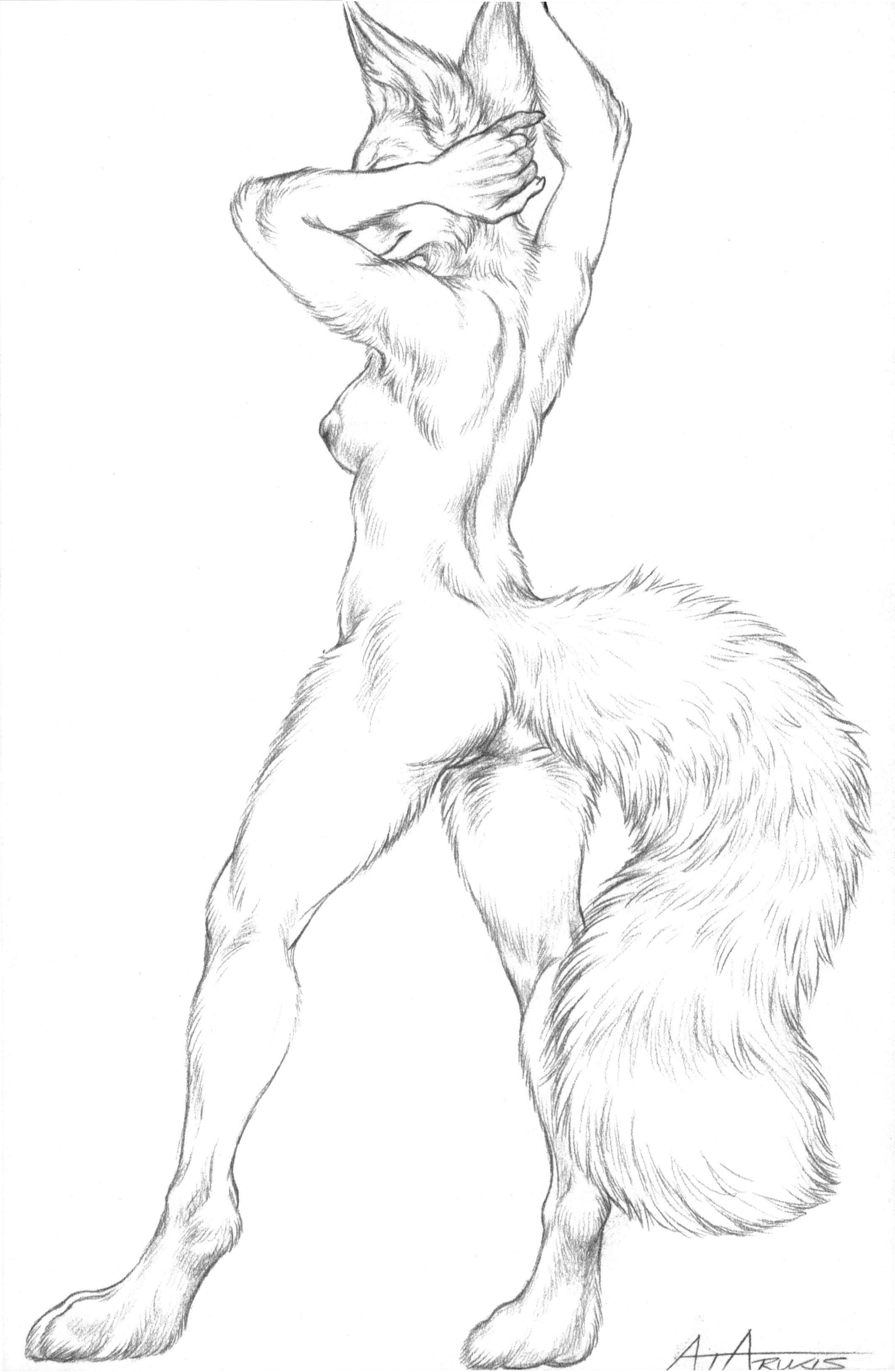

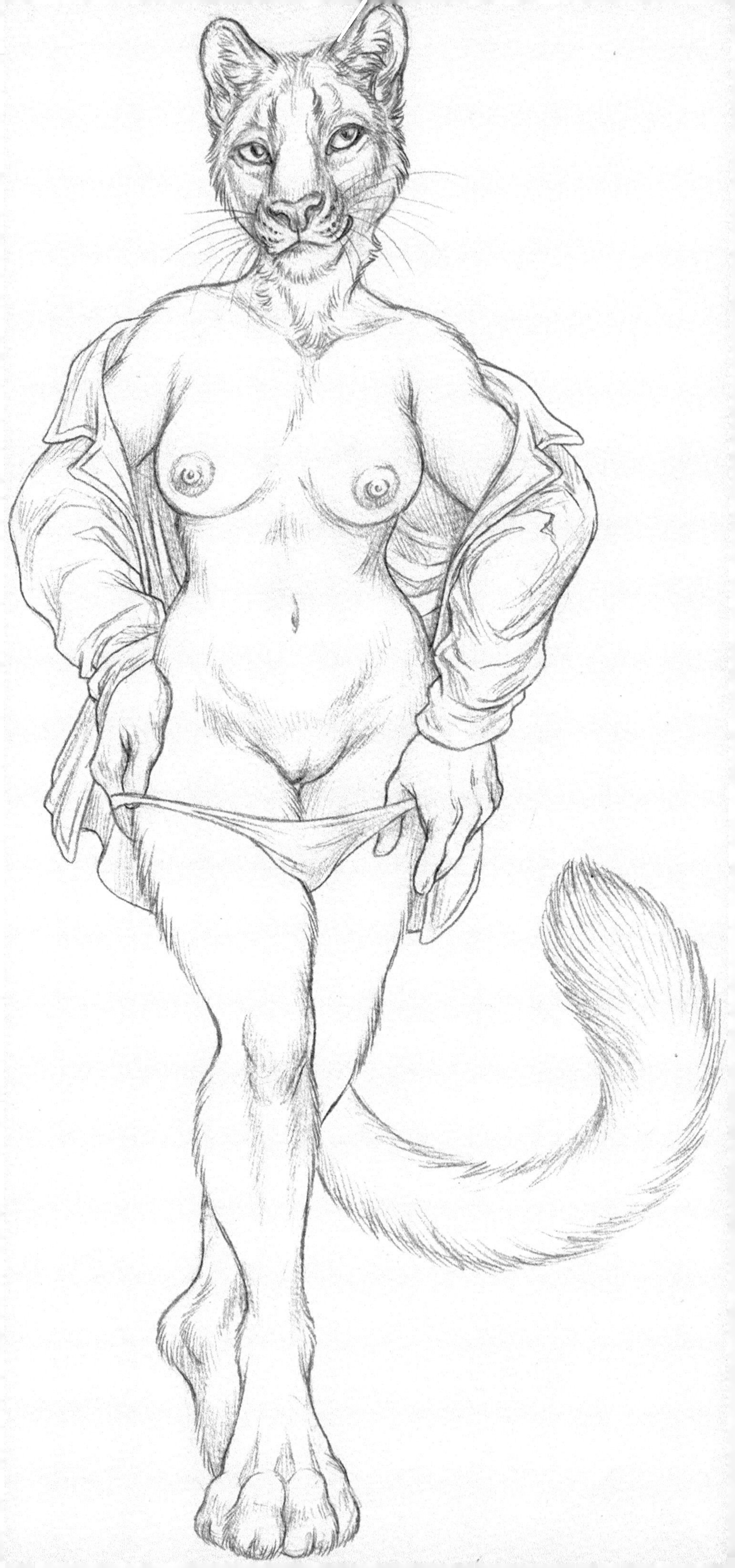

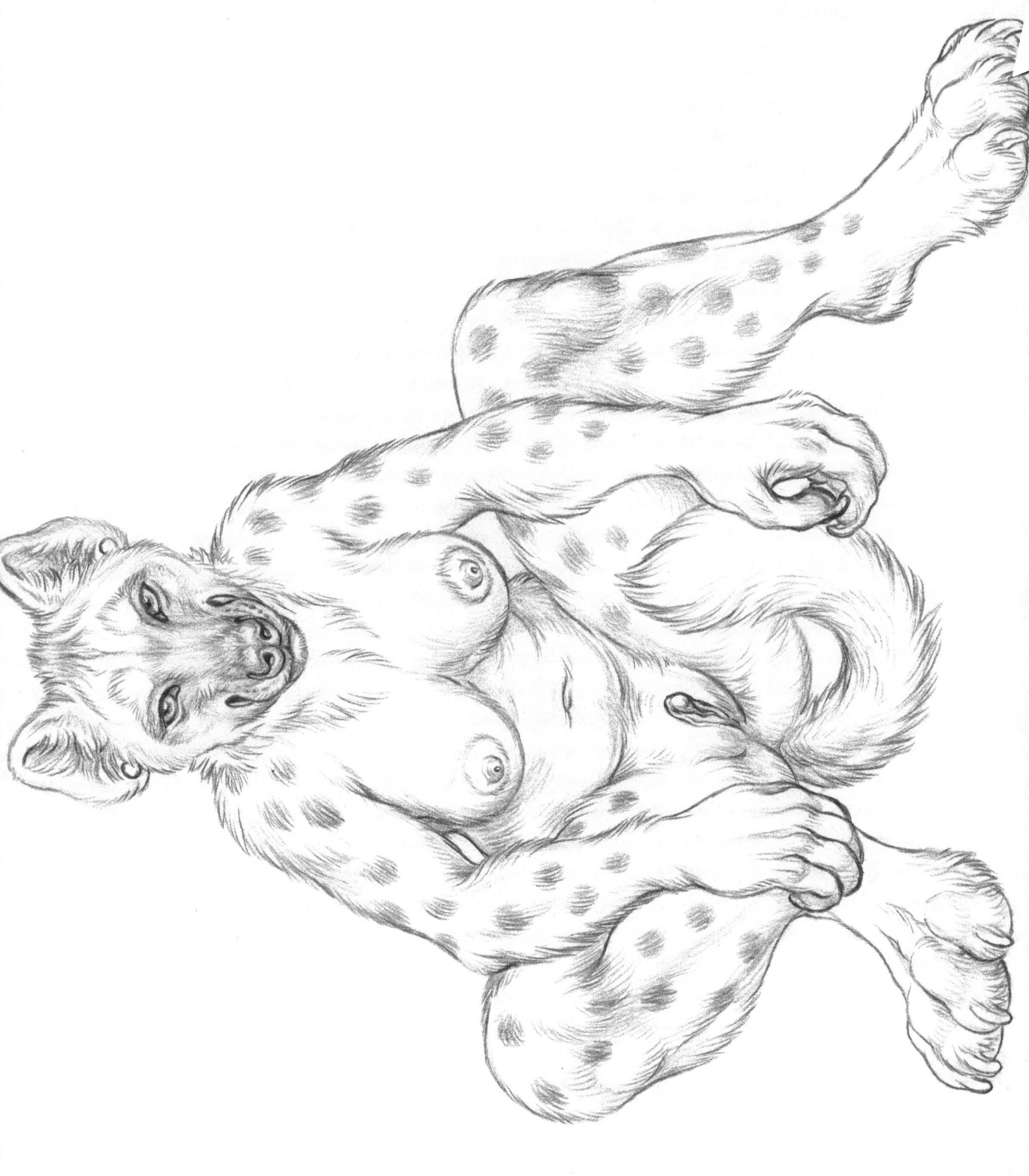

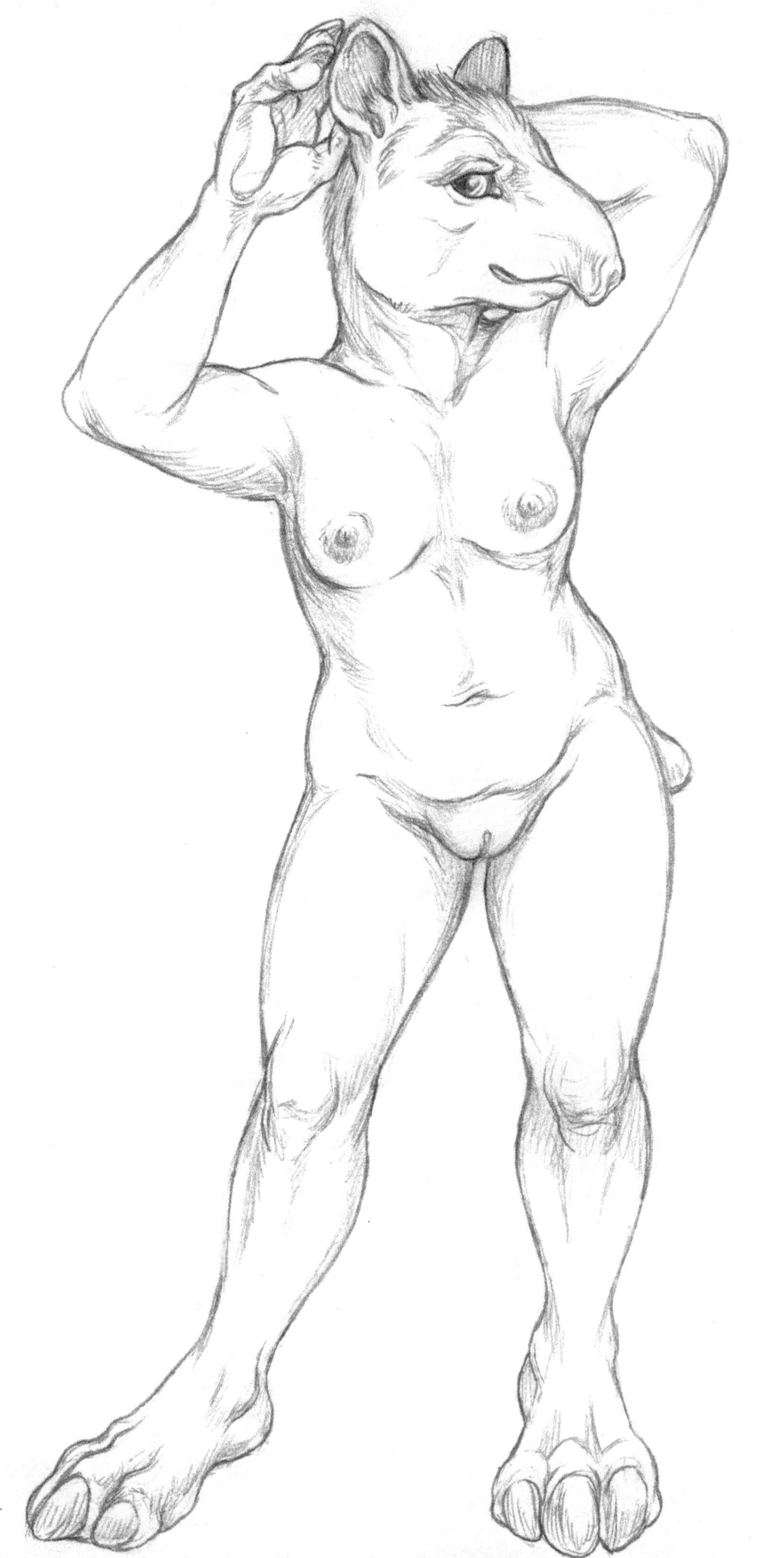

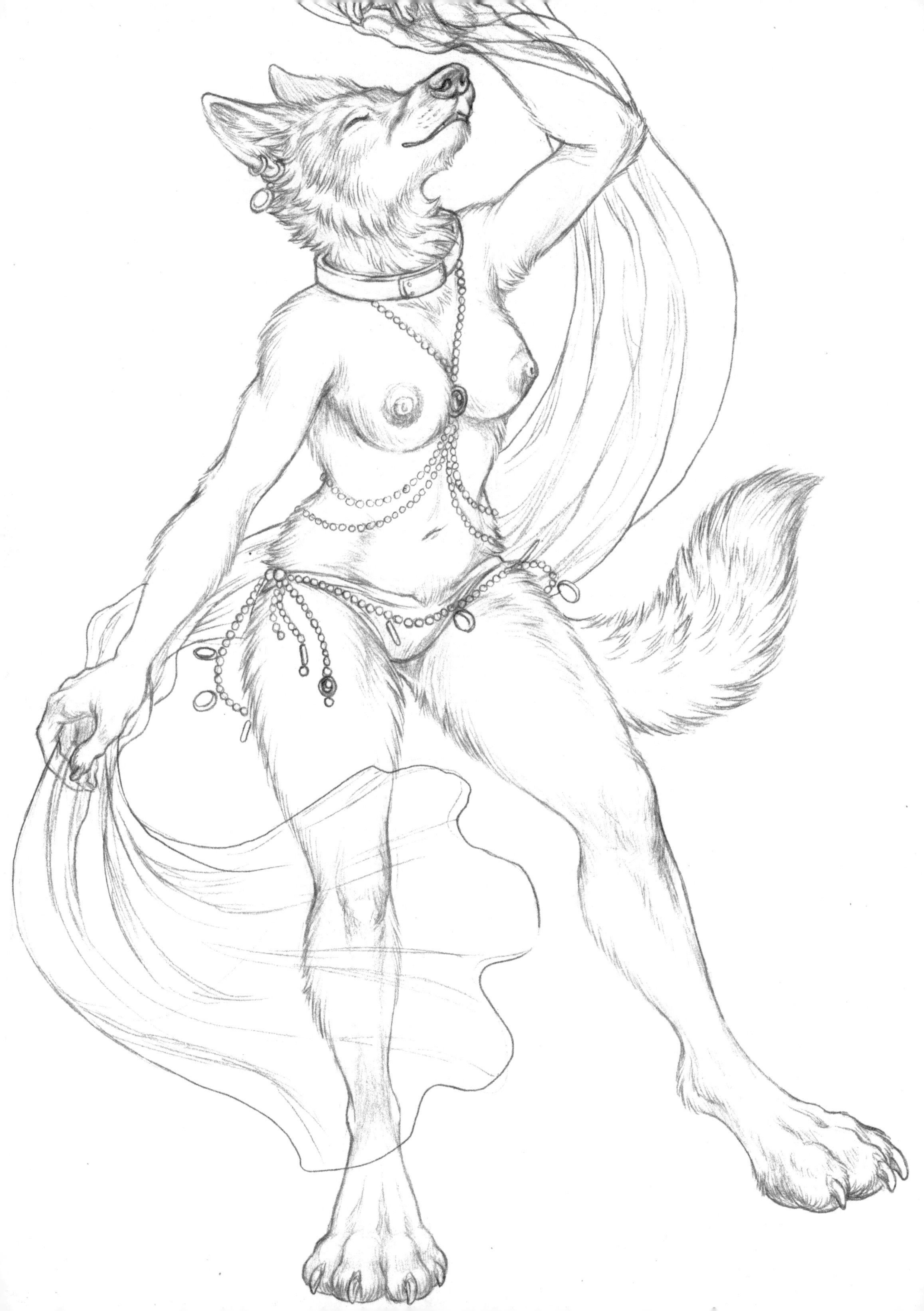

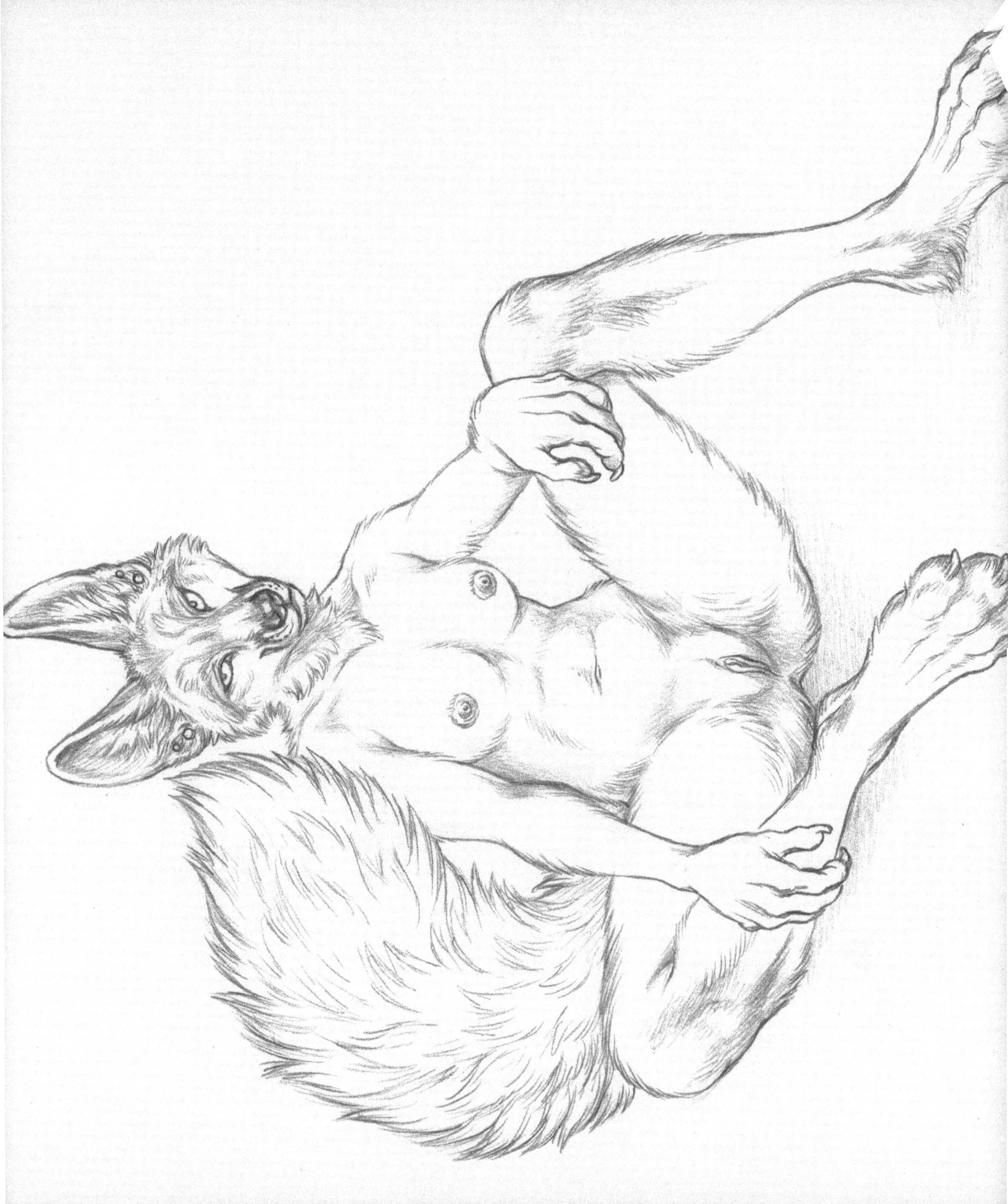

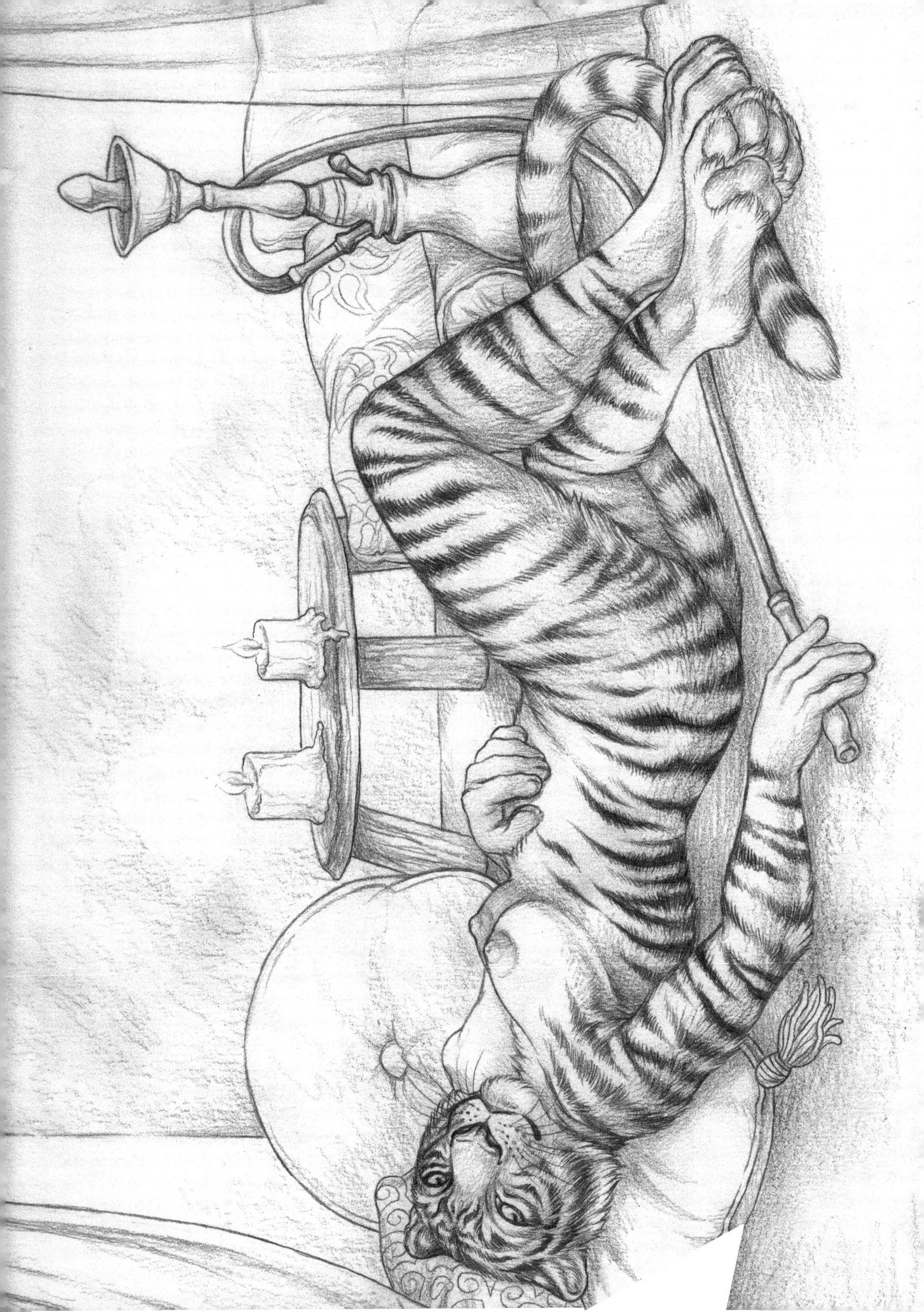

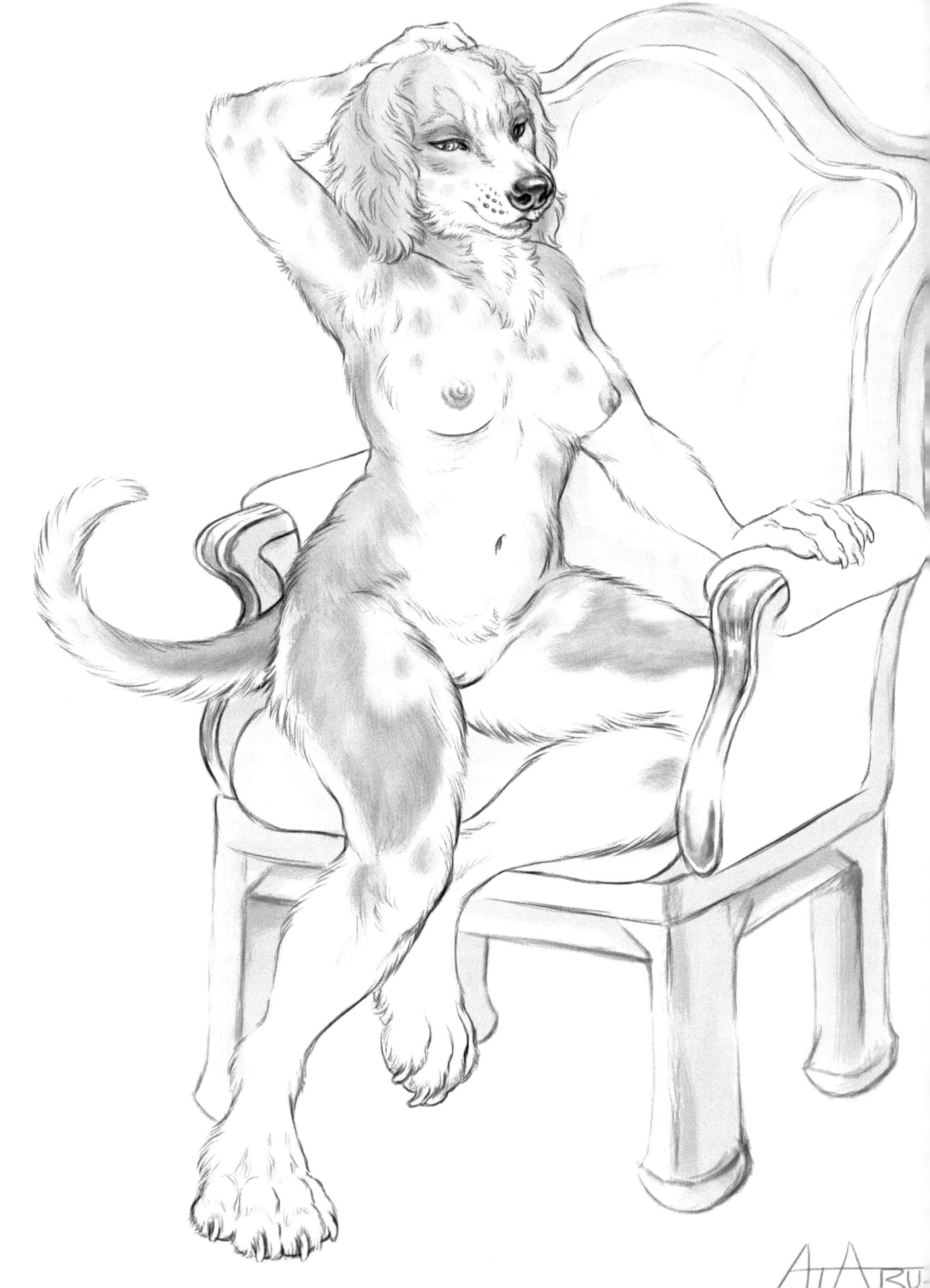

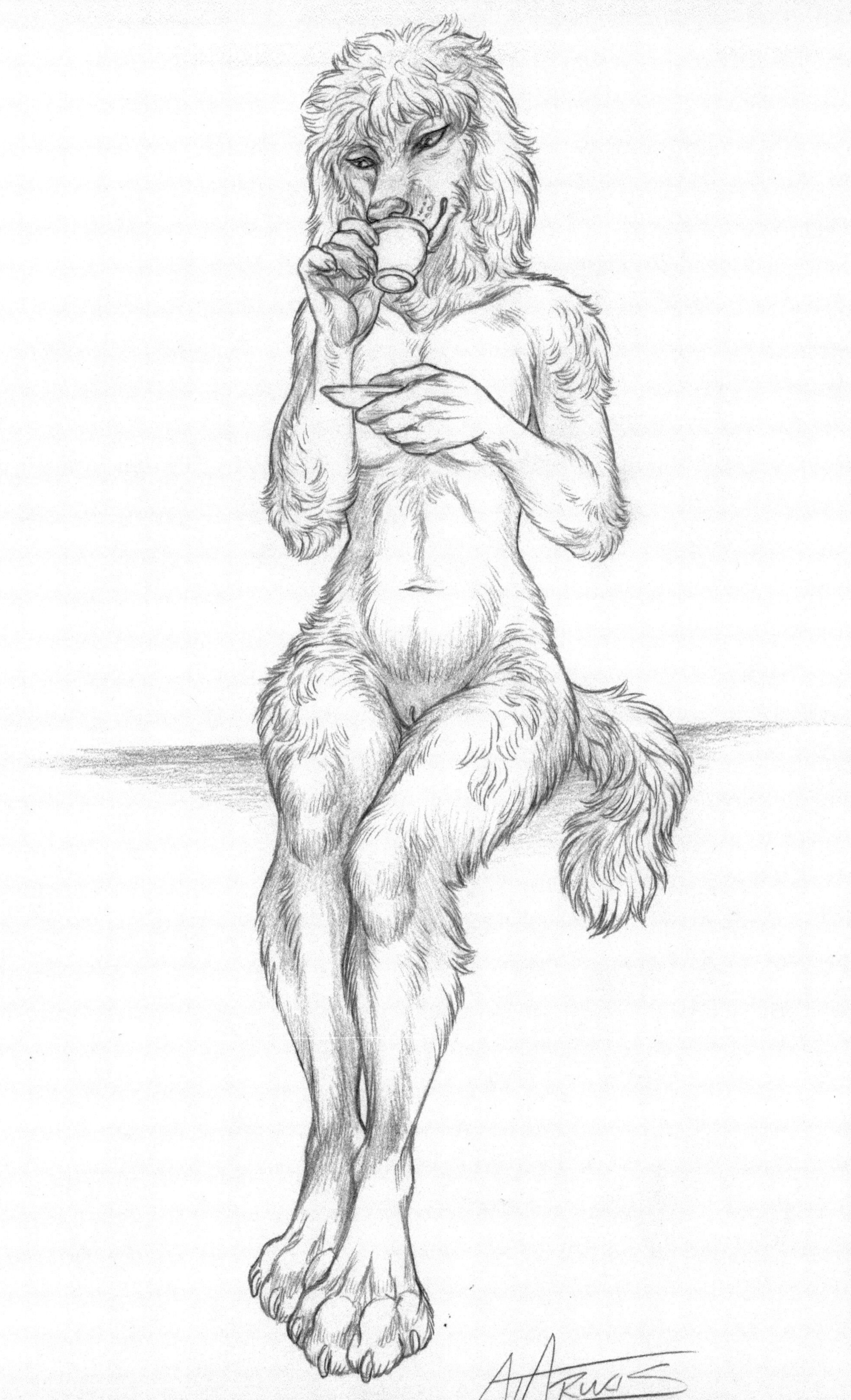

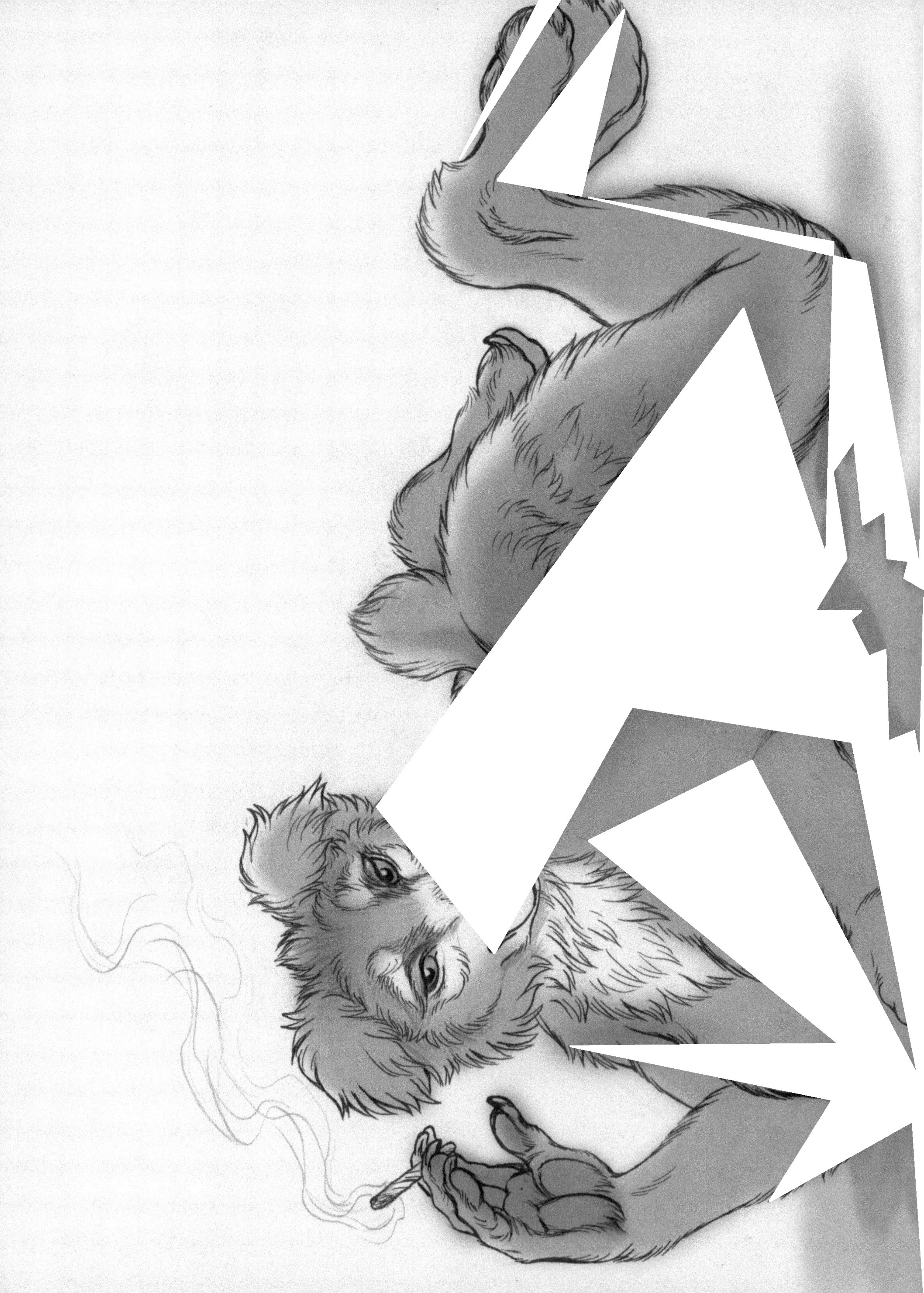

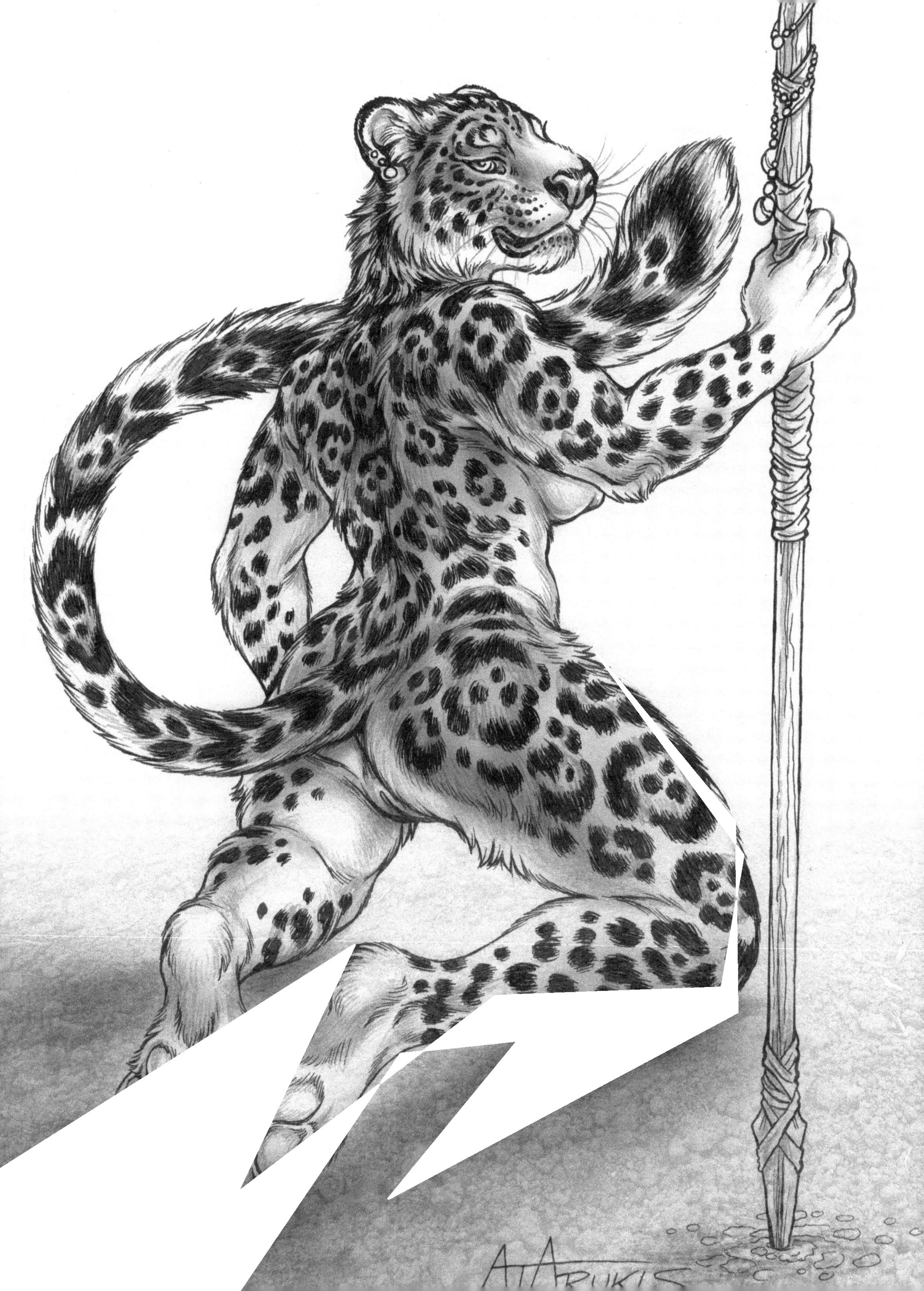

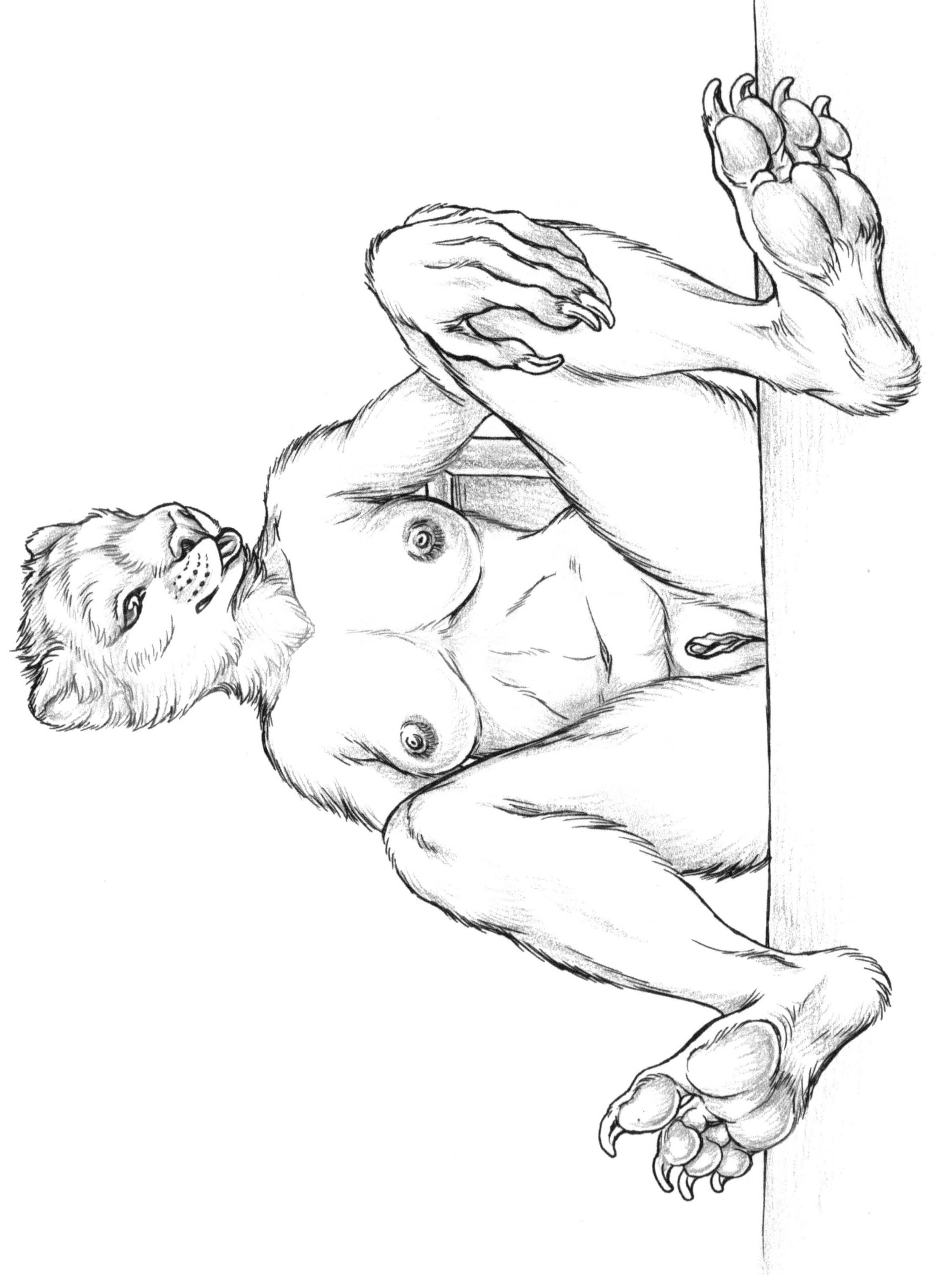

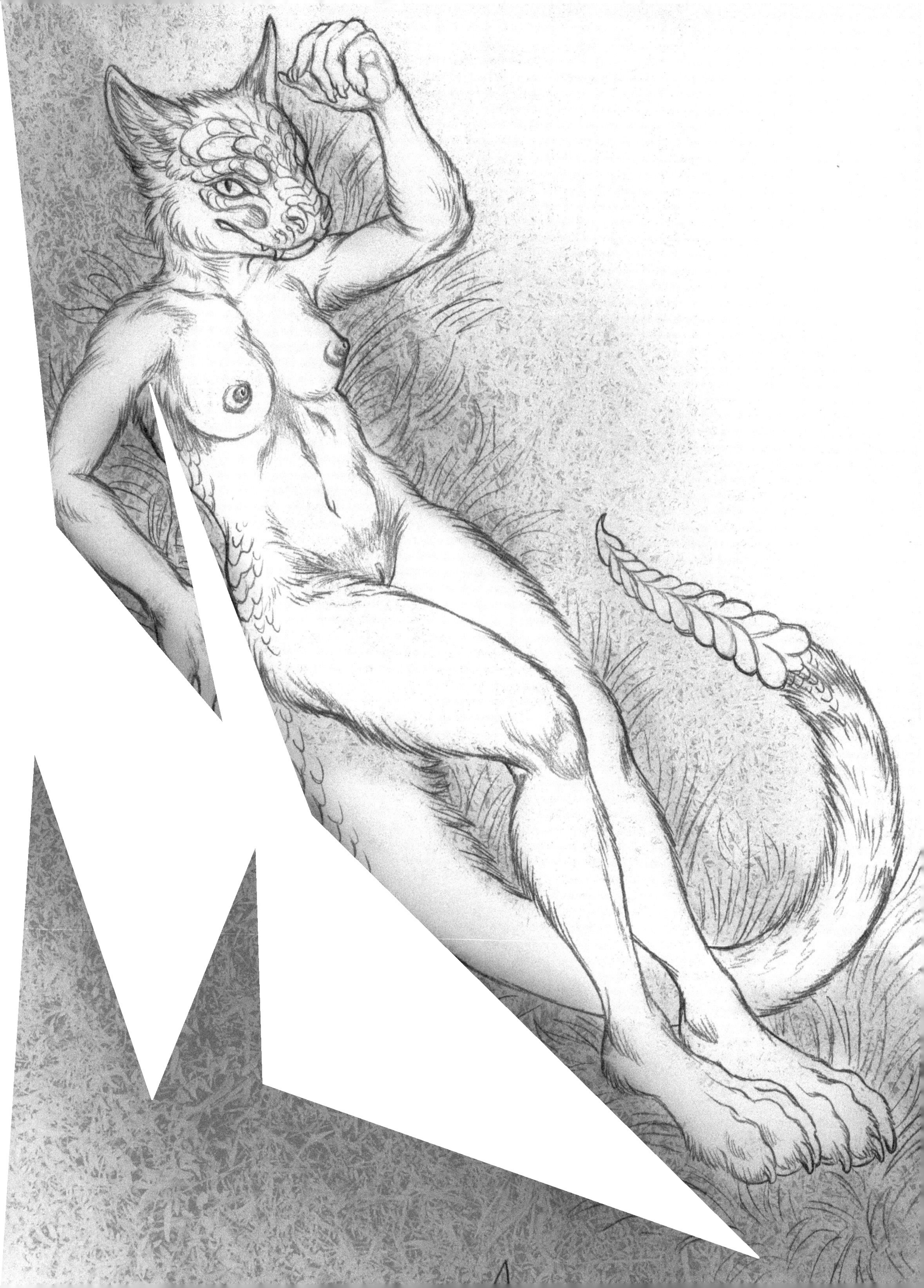

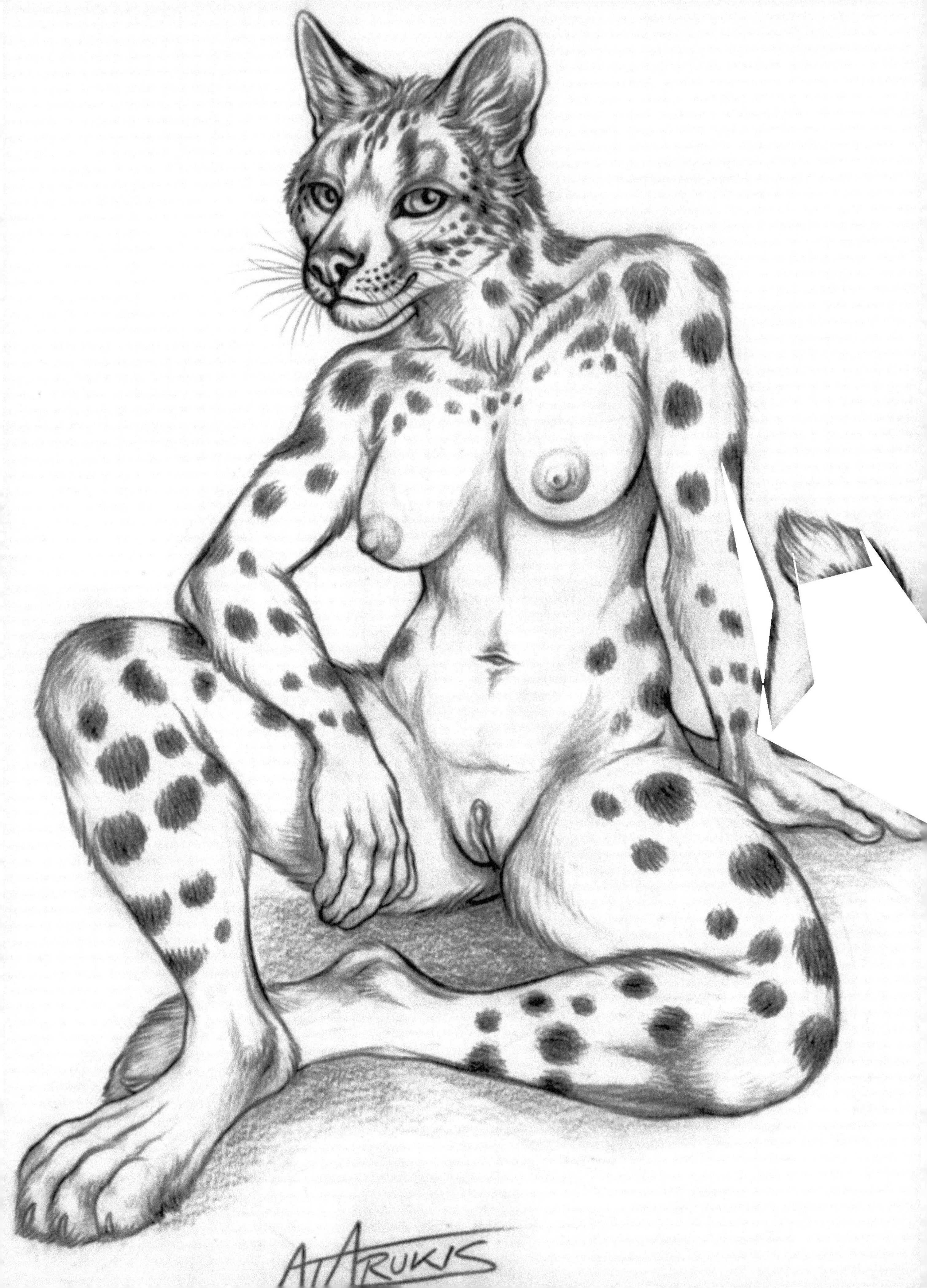

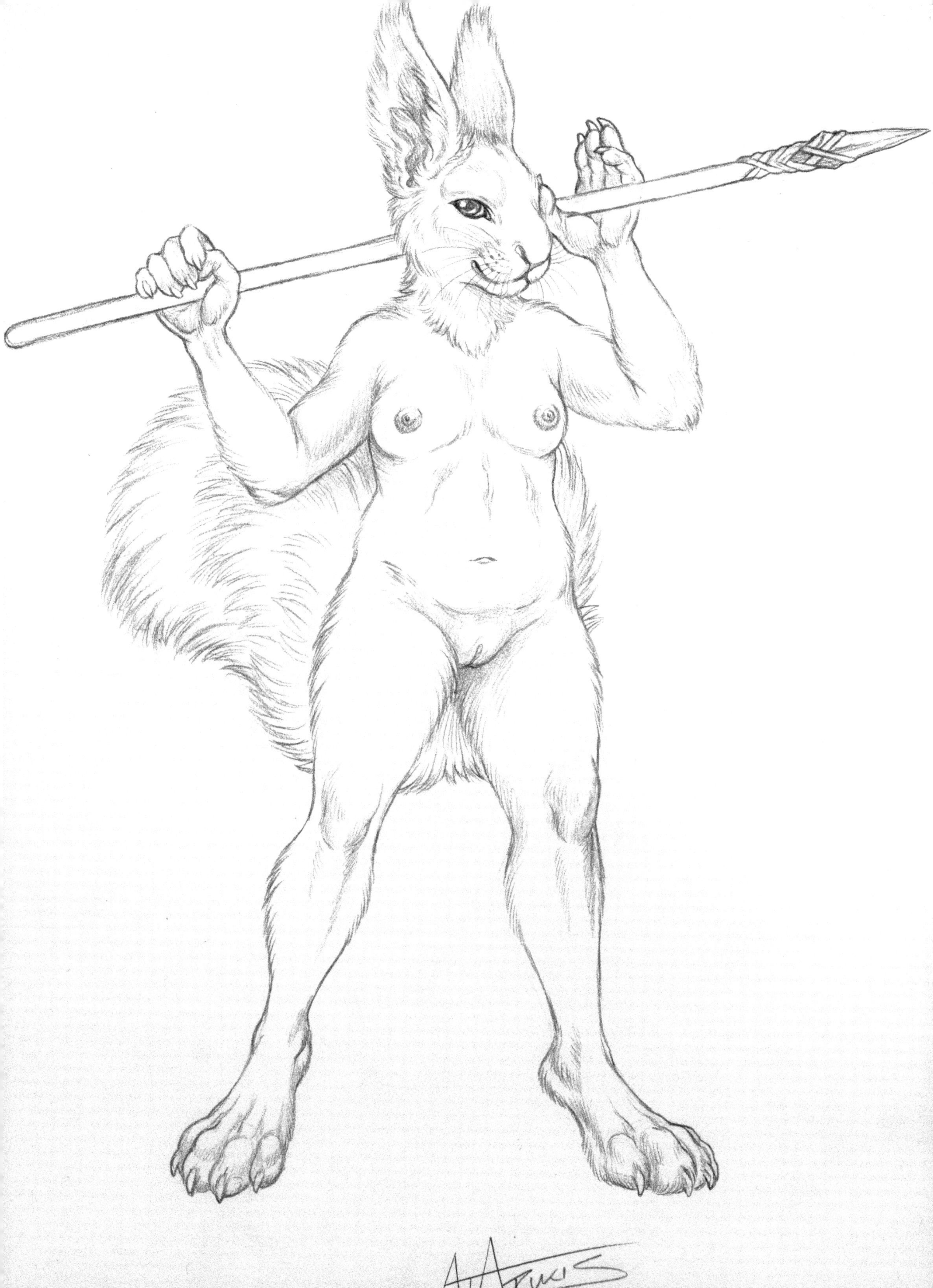

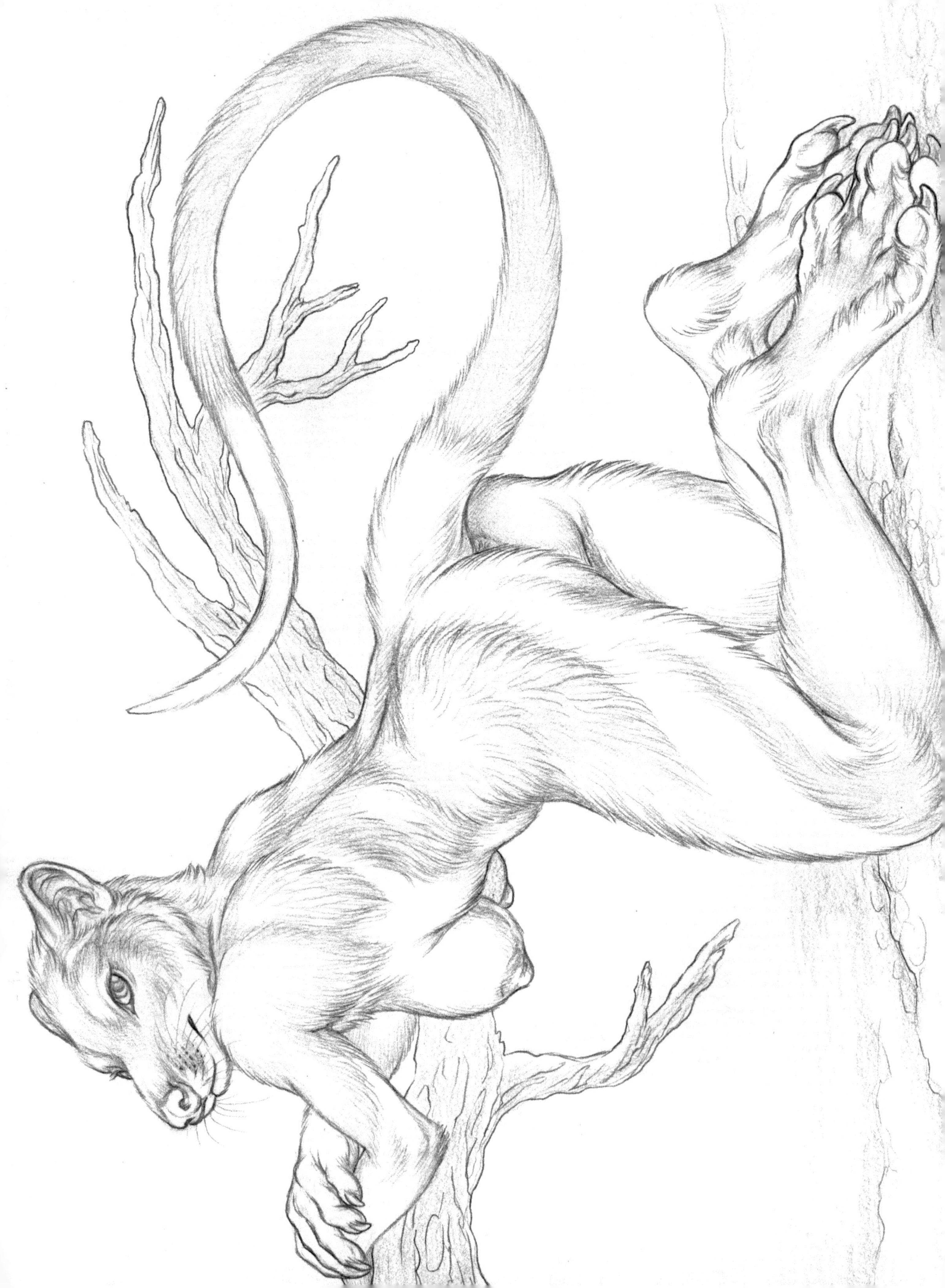

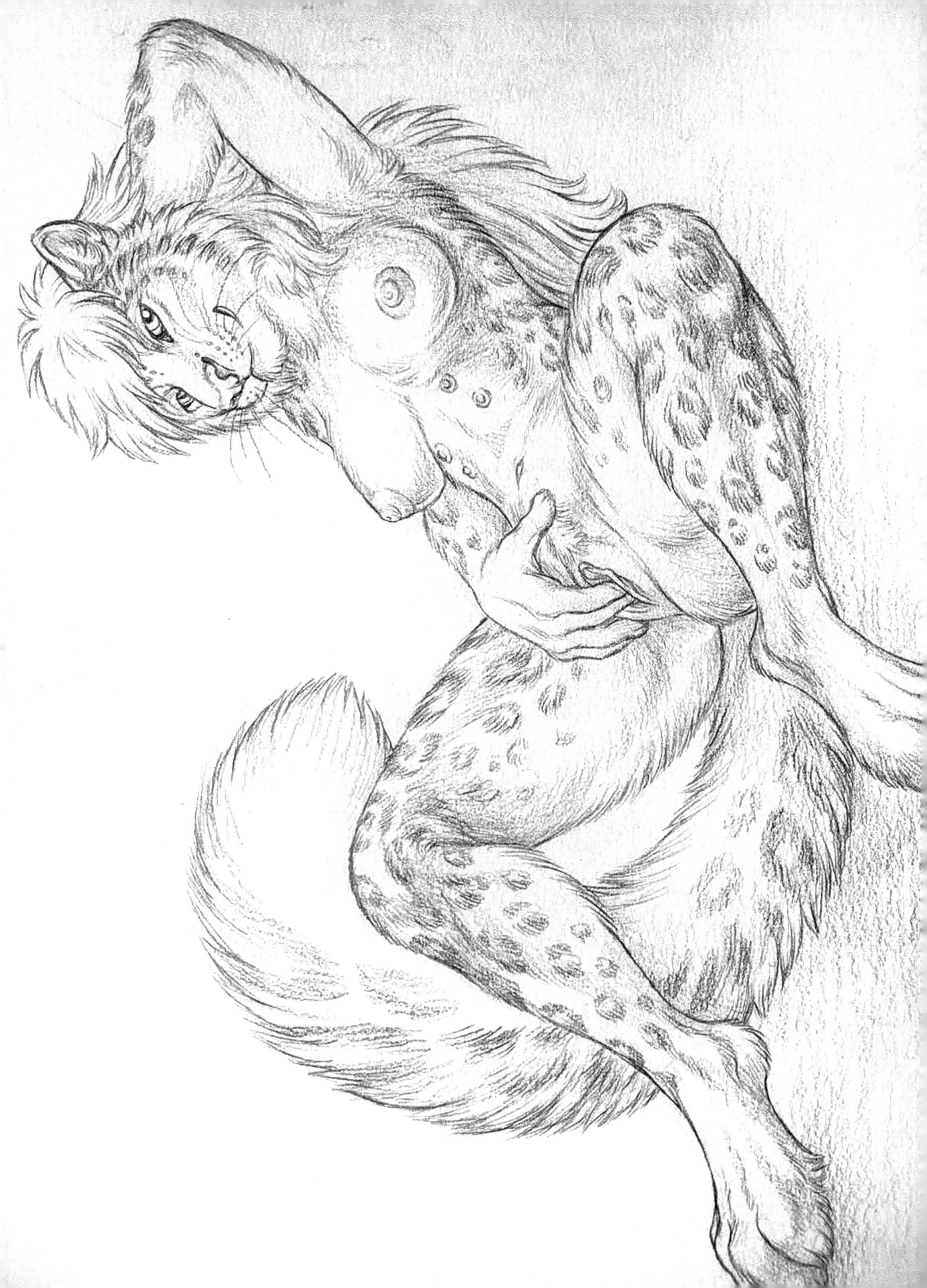

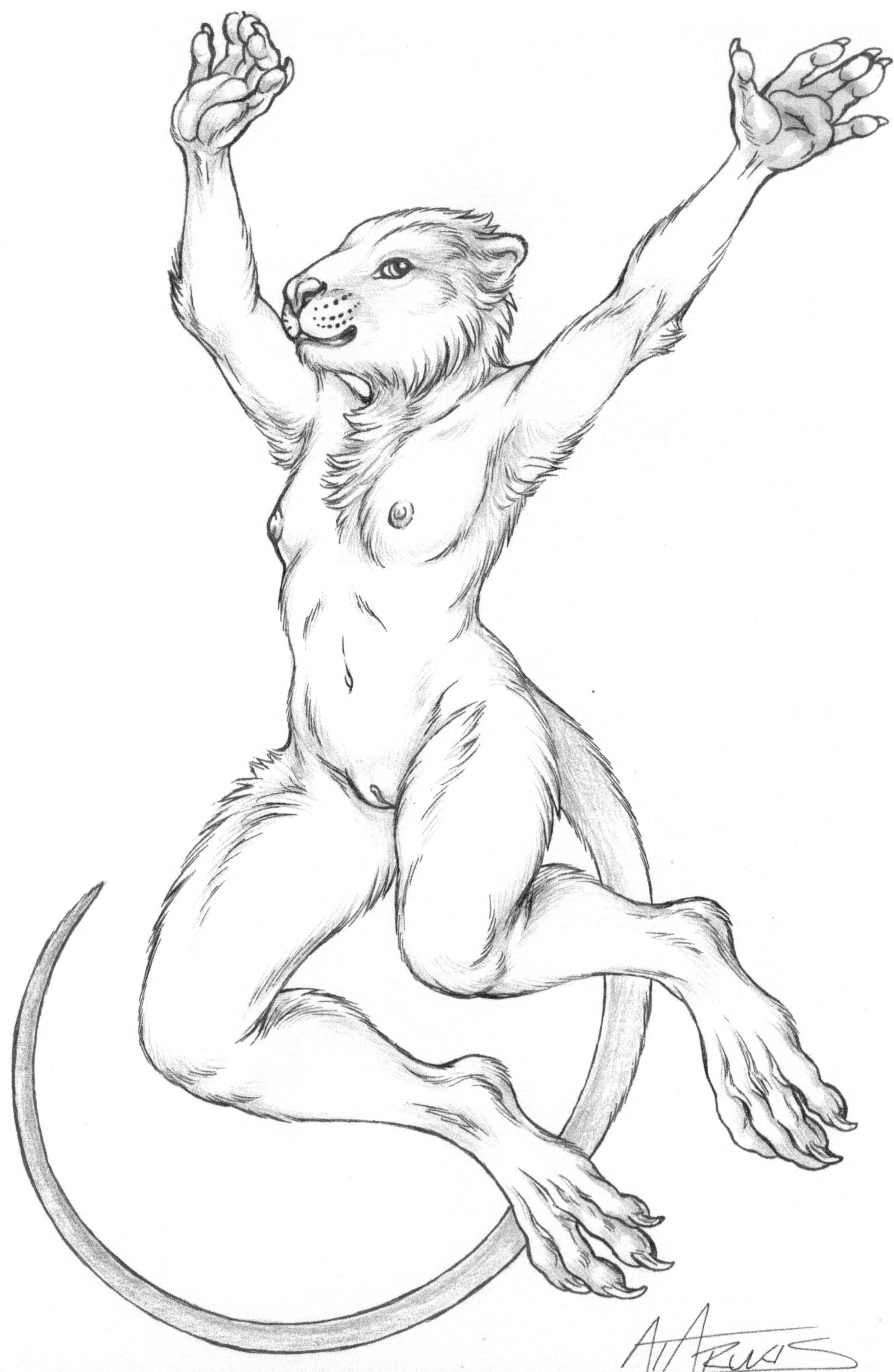

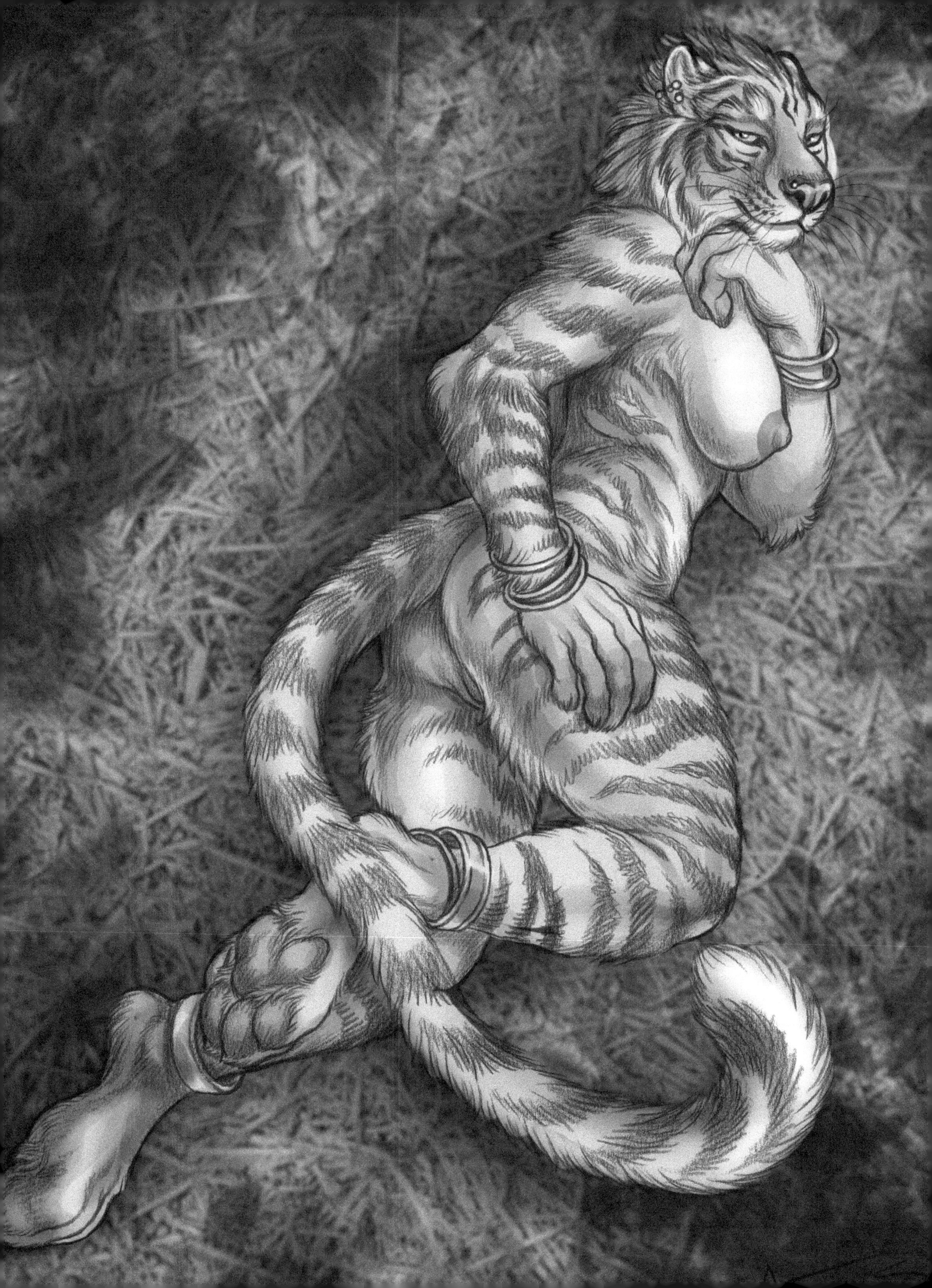

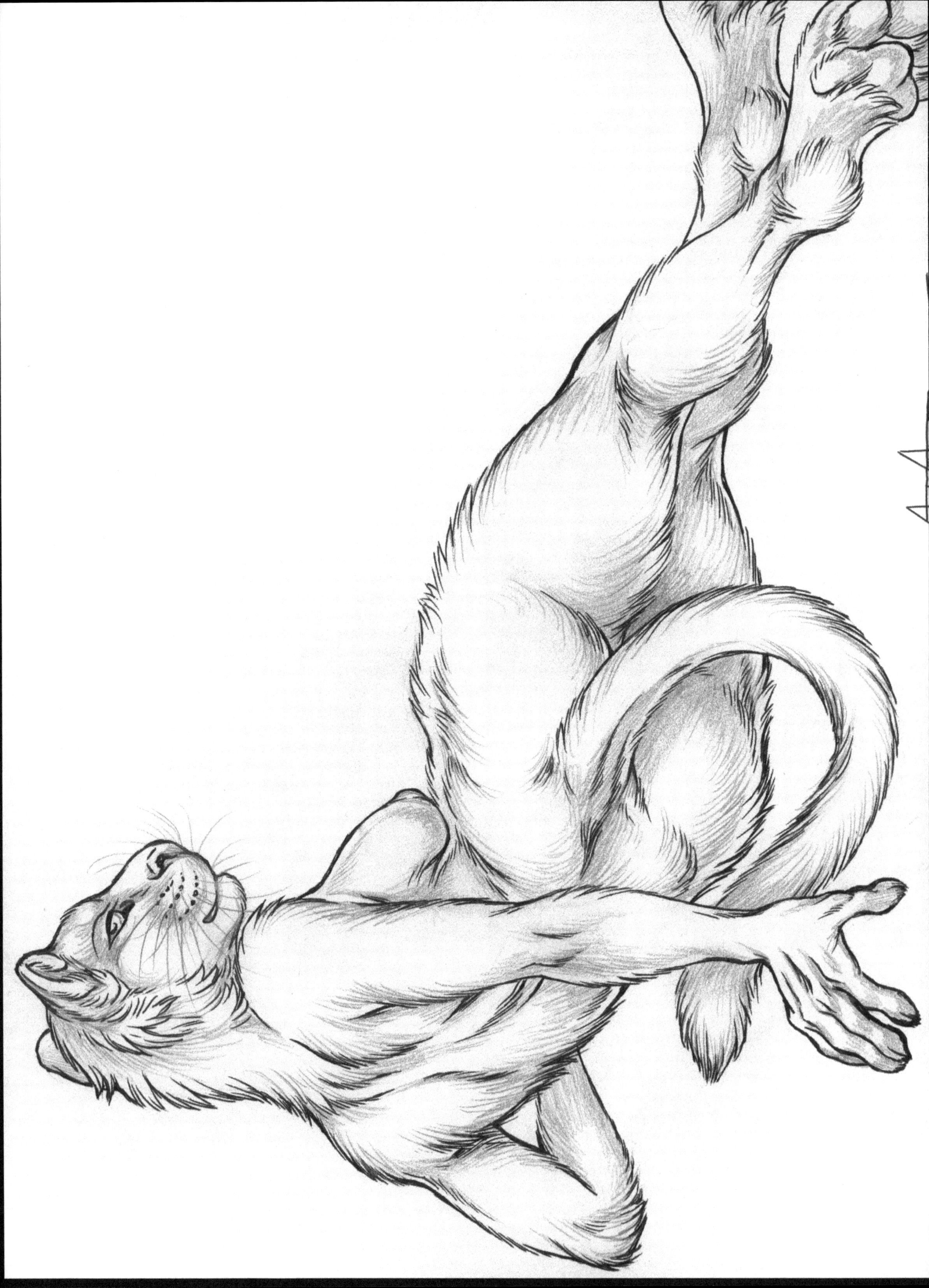

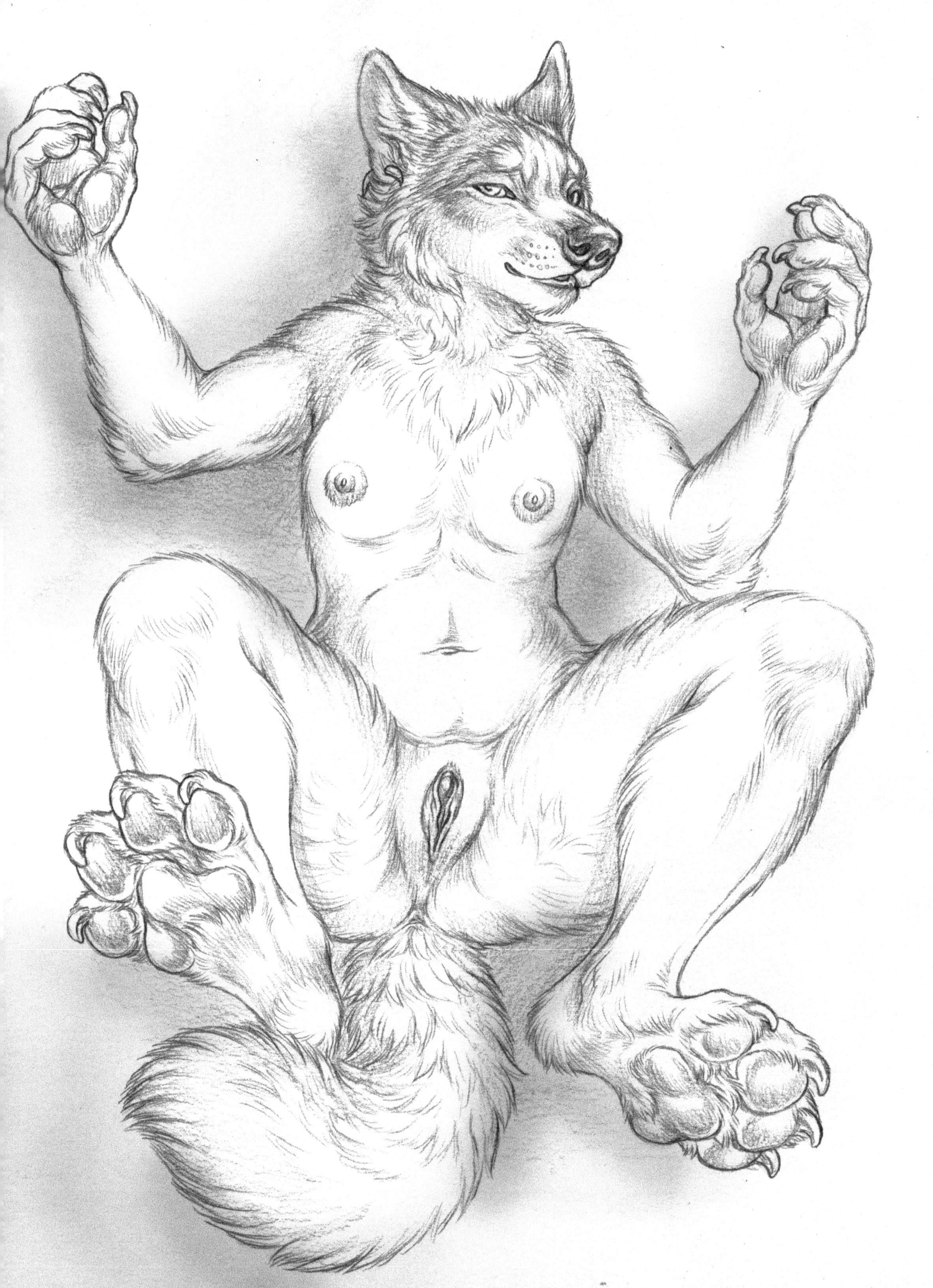

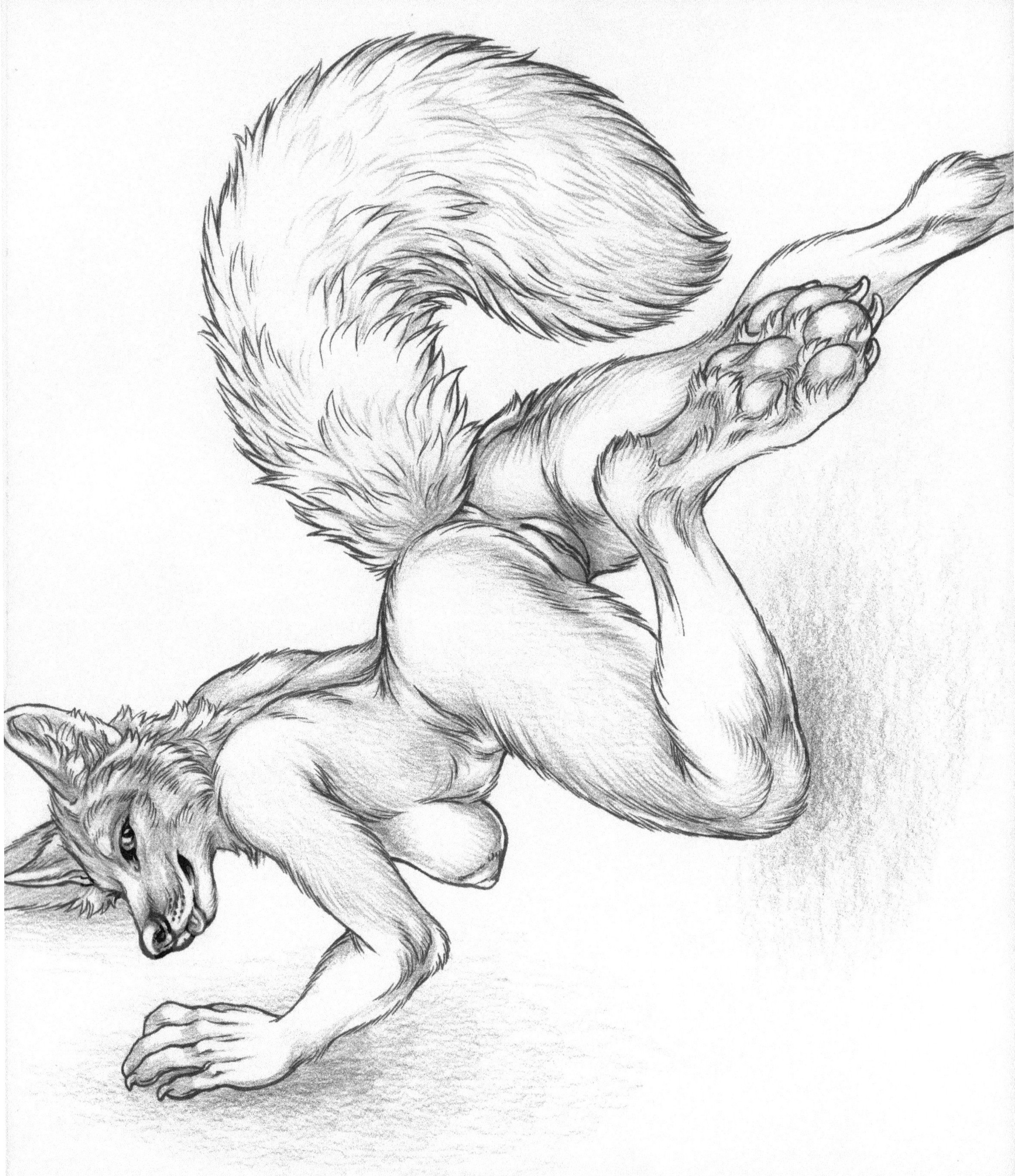

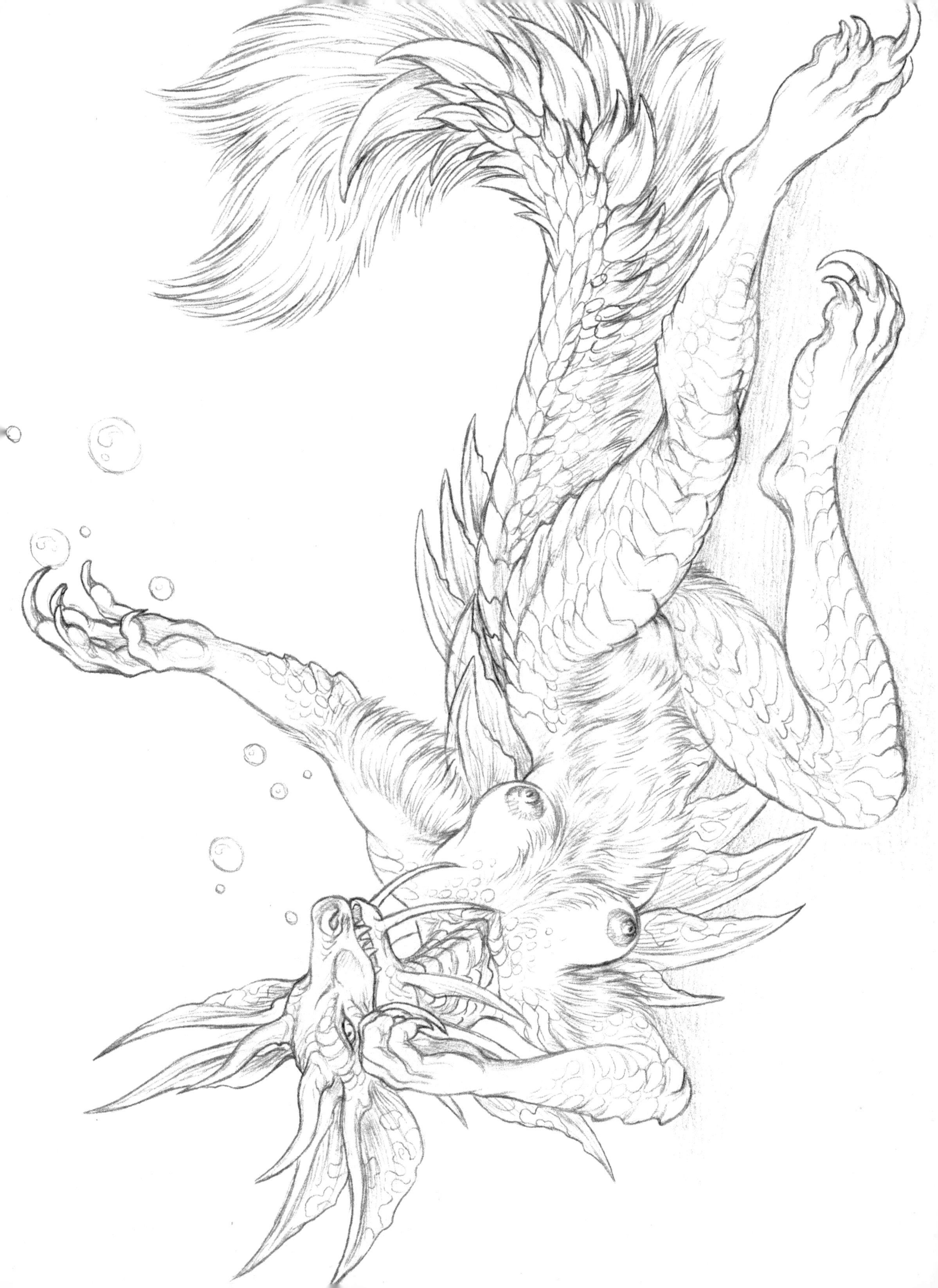

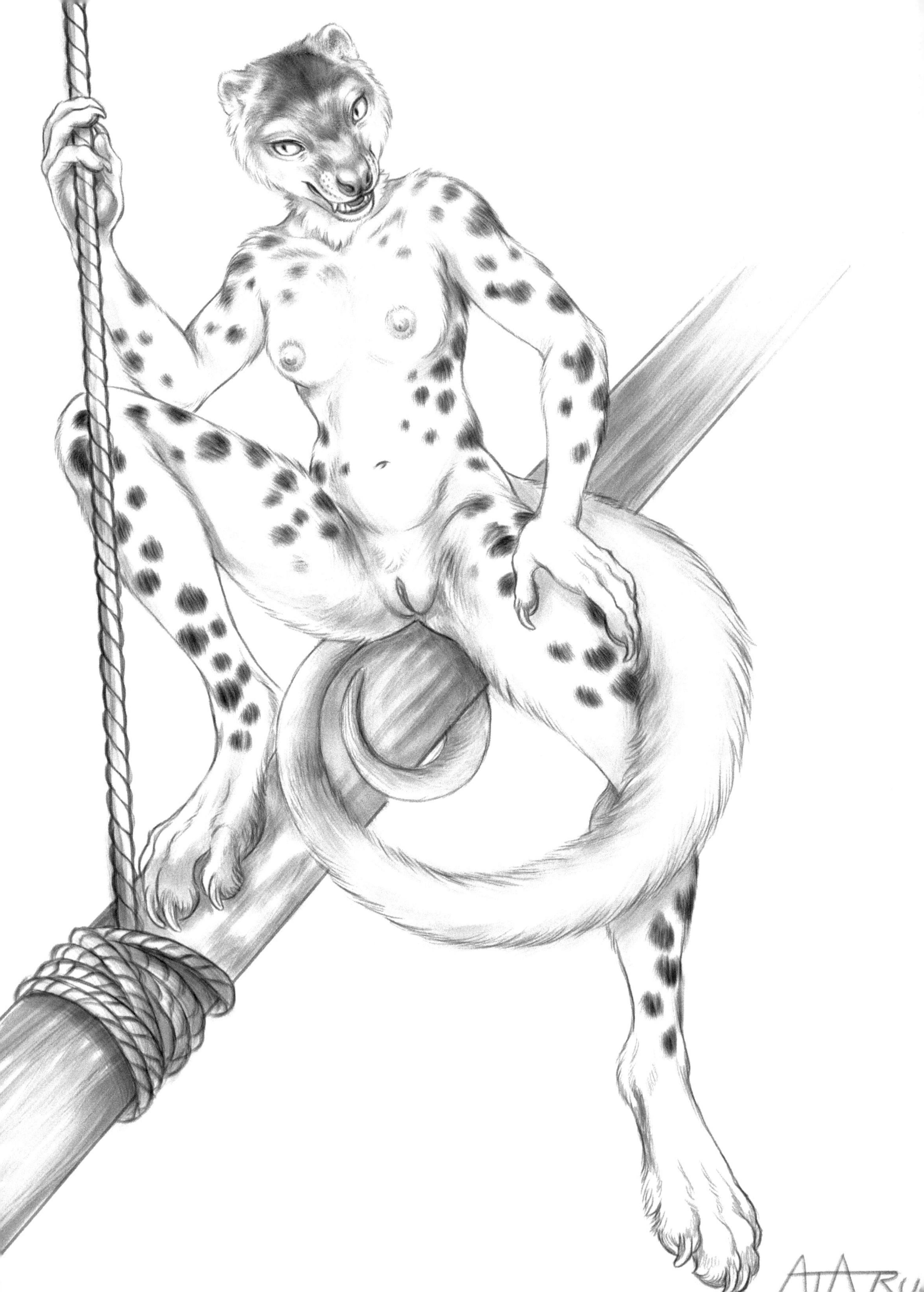

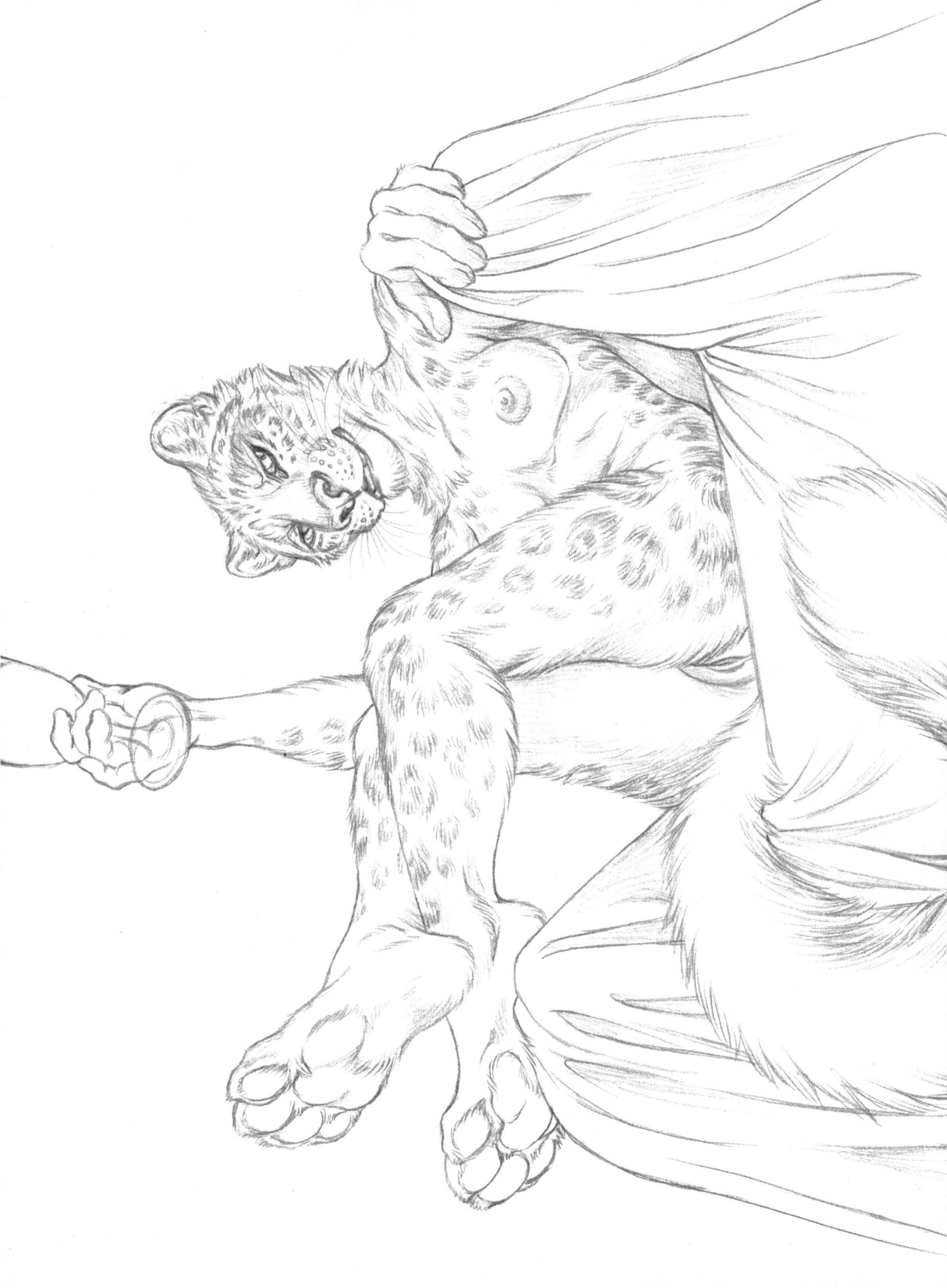